MAGICK AND MISCHIEF

Warlocks MacGregor®

MICHELLE M. PILLOW®

MichellePillow.com

About Magick and Mischief

MAGIC, MISCHIEF AND KILTS!

Kenneth doesn't have room for anything in his life beyond his responsibilities as an immortal warlock and a father. Being a single dad is difficult, especially when that toddler is more powerful than his entire magickal family combined. Standing against forces who want nothing more than to harness his daughter's power takes focus, dedication, and the willingness to put his life on hold. So when the mysterious yet beautiful Andrea appears on his doorstep, he can't help but distrust her.

For two years, Andrea Breaux has been running from a dangerous supernatural force. She's learned to stay on the move, to never allow grass to grow under her feet, and to be suspicious of everyone and everything. When she finds herself in a house surrounded by magicks and a powerful child who would rather she not leave, Andrea isn't sure what to do or if she even wants to go. But staying puts everyone at risk, especially the Scottish hottie in a kilt, Kenneth MacGregor.

Warning: Contains yummy, hot, mischievous MacGregors who are almost certainly up to no good on their quest to find true love. And Uncle Raibeart.

Warlocks MacGregor® Series

SCOTTISH MAGICKAL WARLOCKS

Love Potions

Spellbound

Stirring Up Trouble

Cauldrons and Confessions

Spirits and Spells

Kisses and Curses

Magick and Mischief

A Dash of Destiny

Night Magick

More Coming Soon

Visit www.MichellePillow.com for details.

Author Updates

To stay informed about when a new book is released sign up for updates:

michellepillow.com/author-updates

Note from the Author

The term "warlock" is a variation on the Old English word "waerloga" primarily used by the Scots. It meant traitor, monster, deceiver, or other variations. The MacGregor Clan does not look at themselves as being what history has labeled their kind. To them, warlock means magick, family, and immortality. This book is not meant to be a portrayal of modern day witches or those who have such beliefs. The MacGregors are a magickal class all their own.

As with all my books, this is pure fantasy. In real life, please always practice safe sex and magic(k).

To My Readers

Tabitha Day for my very own skeleton key, sage-lavender smudging stick, and brick dust.

Rachael Messing for your help making reader games and charts.

Thank you both for your generosity.

Chapter One

SOMEWHERE IN MAUREPAS SWAMP, LOUISIANA

Tick, tick, scrrich, tick...

Andrea Breaux kept her back pressed against the wall of the dilapidated home. Light from the electric camping lantern glowed all around her. Remnants hinted at the past in broken furniture pieces and overturned bowls. An empty frame hung at an angle on a wooden wall filled with rot and age. The stilts keeping the creaky floorboards elevated above the swamp below were probably in worse condition. Alligators swam in the murky waters. They'd be impossible to see in the dark if she were to fall through.

None of that scared her. She'd welcome an alligator right about now. At least the creature would be corporeal.

Scrrich, tick, tick...

She had drawn the symbols in the dust on the floor just as she was told. They were to protect her, but she didn't feel very protected.

Tick, tick…

The soft sound moved around the four rooms of the home unhampered by walls—kitchen, then washroom, then bedroom… Andrea closed her eyes tight as the sound entered where she stood in the living room. She tried to remain motionless, holding her breath, willing herself to be invisible.

Tick, scrrich, tick, scr—

The noise stopped.

Andrea kept her eyes closed. Her heart beat so hard that she felt it vibrating up her throat. Her lungs burned until she was forced to draw in air. The sound of her ragged breathing was amplified in the silent home. She tried to keep still, but her legs and arms shook.

I want to be anywhere but here. Anywhere but here.

Go away. Please go away.

Why did they send me?

Andrea knew the answer. She was the only one close enough who could come. This was about saving lives. There was no choice.

Her breathing intensified, and she pressed her lips tightly together to stop her lungs from filling with air. Tears welled in her eyes. It was then she realized the panting noise wasn't all from her.

She peeked through a slit in her lids. The room looked just as it should, dingy and shadow-cast. Andrea turned her head slowly to the side. She couldn't make her body move any faster than that.

Red-rimmed brown eyes met hers from the weathered face of the swamp dweller who'd died over a hundred years ago. The bulk of the spirit's gray hair had been pulled back into a bun. Strands frizzed around her scalp as if the humidity still bothered it even in the afterlife. The woman's head twitched back and forth as her gaze fixated on Andrea.

Tears streamed down Andrea's cheeks. Her mouth opened, but no sound escaped save the ragged pants. She attempted to leave, but fear kept her trapped against the rotted wall.

The spirit's mouth opened wide as her ethereal jaw unhinged. A high-pitched sound shot needles of pain through Andrea's ears, rattling her to the core. With the screech came the wind, a raging storm that slammed the decaying old home. How the structure remained standing, she would never understand for it should have dissolved into a million pieces.

Andrea cried out. She reached to the side, trying to pull herself away since her legs wouldn't move. A fingernail broke against the wall.

"I mean no disrespect, Mama Cecile," Andrea whispered, trying to remember the words she was supposed to say to send the lost spirit into the afterlife. "I mean no…"

The screaming stopped. Cold crept in. By all rights, Andrea should have been dead by now. No one survived an encounter with Cecile.

"I mean no disrespect. I mean no harm," Andrea whispered. "I wish to free you, trapped spirit. Find peace."

The apparition lifted a hand. Andrea watched as it hovered over her chest. Icy-cold fingers pressed between her breasts, sliding past her skin into her body. Cecile seized hold of her heart.

A sharp pain radiated throughout Andrea, but worse than that was the emotional torment. Loneliness and despair filled each gasped breath. A child cried. Panicked shouts came as if from far away, the disembodied echoes spreading throughout the house as if more souls were trapped within the rotting walls.

The storm raged. Wind forced itself through the old slats and swirled the dirt on the floor, ruining the symbols she'd drawn in the dust.

Cecile's eyes became dark pits before filling with fire. Her grip inside Andrea's chest tightened. Flames lit the walls of the home, casting the shadows with an even scarier orange glow. Images flashed, demanding her attention. The house disappeared from her view, replaced by fires raging over a disappearing forest. The air was full of dust and ruin, and the bite of metal flavored her tongue as if the air was filled with tiny shards. The screaming became louder, and she couldn't escape the deafening shrieks. Metal crashed into metal. Horns honked. Loud explosions competed with the cries.

The world was ending, and the fears of the dying human race surged inside her, many moments crammed together until all that was left was a pit filled with sharp, cold pain.

When the vision cleared, Mama Cecile had her face pressed close. Freezing breath hit her heated skin like sheets of ice. Andrea tried to grab Cecile's wrist, but her fingers fell through the spirit like air.

Andrea gasped, feeling faint. No one would come to save her. She was alone, and the fear was so much worse than the pain.

Just as suddenly as the spirit's attack had started, it ended. The cold disappeared and the storm outside lightened. The deep fear, however, did not go away. That remained rooted inside of her.

Tick, tick.

The sound softened...

Tick, tick, scrrich, ti—

…and then disappeared altogether.

Andrea gasped for breath, unable to calm her racing heart. She listened for a long time. The storm continued to let up before finally dissipating. The echoing screams stopped. The house became quiet.

Deathly quiet.

Andrea violently shook as she fell to the floor. She crawled across the creaky old boards toward the electric camping lamp. She caught sight of her reflection in a piece of shiny metal propped up against a broken chair. Blood trails ran from her nose and ears. Her dark brown hair had turned as white as snow.

Coming to the swamp had been a mistake. She should have listened to that nagging feeling in the pit of her stomach the second she was told to go. All the preparation in the world would not have equipped her for a task like this one.

Andrea held the handle on the light and ran toward the front door, hoping the soft glow would be enough to guide her from the uneven porch to the small boat waiting in the dark, alligator-infested swamp.

Chapter Two

GREEN VALLIS, WISCONSIN

Kenneth MacGregor rubbed his eyes, feeling the lingering sting from smoke and heat as if it had just happened. The nightmares were nothing new. His brain seemed intent on reminding him of the past, as if he could forget being tortured while fathering a magickal child in the Appalachian Mountains of West Virginia.

That child was the only good thing to have come from that night—his beautiful daughter. She defined innocence in every way and he would do everything to make sure no one took advantage of her.

His eyes adjusted in the dim light and he felt Jewel wiggling on the bed next to him. They'd fallen asleep for a much-needed nap, and he was grateful the girl had finally let him rest. No one had to tell him that being a single parent was difficult. He'd been living it for years. Even now that he was home with his parents, aunts and uncles, siblings and cousins, he still lived it. His family tried to help when they could, but it wasn't the same as having a partner. All decisions, all responsibilities fell onto his shoulders. At times it was isolating and lonely.

Kenneth knew he should be happy to be home. He'd spent twenty-five years hiding and during that time he'd missed his close-knit family. In many ways the MacGregors had always been the poster children for codependent relationships —warlocks who stayed together, moving from place to place in an effort to hide their immortality, feeding each other's magick, up in each other's business.

They originally came from Scotland, so many hundreds of years ago that he'd forgotten what it felt like before the days of technology and science. Just as people evolved to have dark hair or blue eyes, his family had evolved to possess magickal abilities and immortality. Well, immortality insomuch as no one physically killed them. They could still die, just not from natural old age or human sickness.

From Scotland they'd lived around Europe before coming to America. Back then the land had been open and untouched. They witnessed the so-called progress of modern times. The world became smaller, connected by telegraphs, then phones, then the internet. The family had lived at Southern plantations, New York penthouses, and every imaginable location in between. Now they'd settled in the middle of Wisconsin in a Georgian mansion overlooking the town of Green Vallis from atop a hill.

Kenneth wasn't sure how his brother, Erik, had found the home, but it was a remarkable location. This was a place born to feed magick. As a warlock, he needed to borrow energy from nature to fuel his powers. Green Vallis was full of nature. But what made the town special flowed beneath the surface. Ley lines converged to create a powerful nexus. His family had discovered them a few years back. Why they emerged now was a mystery.

The ley lines also meant the town was full of danger. The MacGregors weren't the only ones drawn to the powerful location. That made it unsafe. Though they'd moved to Wisconsin after he'd disappeared, those kinds of dangers were one of the reasons he'd hid from the family while trying to raise his daughter.

At first glance, Green Vallis looked like just another small town with red brick streets half paved over with concrete and historical buildings boasting ages engraved on exterior placards. It amused him that a hundred years was considered historical, but such was American history.

Being away from the MacGregor dynamic had taught him a self-reliance he'd not had before. Kenneth had always thought of himself as independent, but when adversity happened, he'd been able to run home to the safety of his family. His problems were always solved for him.

Until the birth of his daughter, Margareta.

He'd never imagined himself as a parent, but one night in a West Virginia dive bar had changed everything. His questionable decisions had resulted in more than a moonshine hangover. Wild, drunken sex had quickly turned depraved and resulted in a scarred chest, a nine-hour pregnancy, and an induction into the level of responsibility for which a man like him had not been prepared.

His daughter should have been around twenty-five years old, getting a grip on her magick, branching out into adulthood, maybe falling in love for the first time. He should be running off boyfriends and giving career advice. Instead, her infant body rested in his arms. This was the third time she'd been reborn, the fourth time he'd been through teething and diaper changes. When he looked at her, he saw the three incarnations that had come before and it broke his heart—Margareta, Alice, and Jewel.

Margareta had been named after his ma.

Alice had been named for *Alice's Adventures in Wonderland*, which was her favorite book when she was Margareta.

Jewel because that is what she was to him, the most precious of jewels.

He grieved for her past lives, able to recall the feeling of having her die in his arms only to be reborn in fire.

This was her fourth life. He'd named her Margareta Alice Jewel MacGregor, hoping the combination of the names would somehow fuse her together. Maybe this time she would live a full life.

Maybe.

But doubtful.

The family called her Jewel, because that was who she had been when they'd met her for the first time.

Jewel's mother had been a phoenix. Geneva used him for a death ritual. Giving birth and passing on her curse had been the only way to end her own life. He never wanted Jewel to feel that desperate. If he managed to get her to adulthood and her magick stabilized, he wanted her to find happiness and purpose in that life.

Geneva must have known he came from a family of warlocks. That was the only reason he could discern why she'd picked him. The scars she'd put on Kenneth's chest, painfully carved into his flesh, kept him immune to their daughter's great powers.

"I should have seen the damage in her," Kenneth whispered to his sleepy child. The soft cheeks and quivering lip brought back memories as if no time had passed from her first birth. He'd been terrified. He remembered thinking he'd be less scared to fight a den of hungry vampires than holding his fragile infant daughter. "Your ma was a troubled woman. The truth is, I don't know if she could have loved ya. She didn't love me. She didn't know me."

"Ba, da, ba," the baby babbled, her eyes opening and closing, as if trying to tell him something.

"I lied to ya about that in your last lives. I shouldn't have. Maybe understanding what your mother was, her struggles, her failings, her pain, will help ya get through the life ahead of ya."

Jewel's eyes opened and he saw a tiny glint of flames circling her irises. A sick feeling filled him as the first sign of her powers became visible. The magick came much earlier than he wanted. Actually, he'd be happy if it never came. The powers would burn inside his daughter like fire over a dry forest—consuming everything until there was nothing left but ash and another rebirth.

There was no greater fear, or sorrow, than this.

In a panic, he reached into her diaper bag and fumbled until he found two metal bands. Kenneth took the bracelets and clamped them around the child's ankles, forcing the metal to bend and overlap so they wouldn't fall off. The flames extinguished into a smoky haze.

"Your grandmother—your ma's ma—gave ya these and ya can never take them off. She's a mountain witch. Her magick should balance the phoenix powers. Maybe this time ya won't…"

The pain rolling over his chest was too much and he couldn't bring himself to say the words out loud. No parent should have to watch their child die over and over again. Each time Jewel had been reborn, her personality had changed and she was a different version of herself. The bracelets were supposed to align her personalities into one but she would not remember her past. They looked like two tiny shackles against her soft skin.

Being a father was all that mattered. From the first moment Kenneth had pulled his daughter from the ashes of her mother, it had been love.

The smell of her head, the grip of her hand on his finger, that first twitch of her mouth, it all marked him. He knew he'd give his life to protect her.

That didn't mean he felt whole. There was a missing piece inside of him that yearned to be filled. He wanted a partner, someone he could lay next to at night and talk about the day. His brothers had recently married and seeing the couples together made that ache all the more real.

"Your ma must have chosen me because of my immortality, so I could always take care of ya when ya flame out because she knew she wouldn't be here to do it." Kenneth closed his eyes. It was a curse all its own. Though the bracelets should work, the truth was he could lose Jewel at any moment and it was his eternity to be ready to re-raise her when that happened.

As painful as it was, he could do nothing else.

This was his fate.

This was what it meant to be a parent.

Kenneth had spent each of the child's lives hiding her from the supernatural world, protecting her. Phoenix powers were rare and coveted. In the wrong hands, Jewel could do much damage. It was why he'd hidden her from his supernatural family—not that he expected them to use his daughter for ill gain, but because evil beings tended to follow the MacGregors wherever they went.

Before Jewel's latest rebirth, his sister Malina had cast a spell to bring him home. It wasn't the first time she'd tried, but it was the first time it had worked. Malina had the unfair advantage of being married to a luck demon. They'd gathered enough good luck in Vegas to draw six-year-old Jewel from where they were hiding in Oklahoma to Wisconsin, thus forcing Kenneth to return to the family.

After twenty-five years away, Kenneth felt out of sync with the rest of them. He tried to explain his concerns to his ma, but Margareta MacGregor waved them away, unable to see past her excitement over her first grandchild. Traditionally, his immediate family always lived under the same roof, and it was expected he'd stay in the mansion with them. The rest of the warlock clan were slowly moving into town, taking over apartment buildings and buying up real estate.

Despite his mother's wishes, Kenneth would not be staying. The moment he'd been waiting for had finally arrived. With the emergence of Jewel's phoenix powers, it was time for him to take her and disappear. He didn't know where they would end up, which meant he could not slip and give hints away.

Hopefully his ma would understand and have some comfort knowing he was alive. It wouldn't be like last time when he'd disappeared with no word. She'd have closure.

She'd also be pissed as hell.

His ma would have to get over it. He would do whatever was best for Jewel.

Kenneth hooked the diaper bag over his shoulder and eased the baby against his chest. He would not risk being seen with luggage. Everything he needed could be replaced on the road.

He hurried down the wide staircase toward the front hall with his hand pressed against Jewel's back. She'd been a fussy sleeper this time around and one cry would sound an alarm. If it wasn't his ma and his aunt Cait hovering, it was his uncle Raibeart.

More than once Kenneth had caught his uncle in a tiara with a pink tutu tucked over his kilt, balanced over the side of the crib whispering, "Remember your uncle Raibeart, princess. I'm the fun one. Our tea parties are waiting."

Jewel would never lack for love if they stayed. But it didn't change the fact that those who loved her were magickal, and that magick drew danger.

Kenneth stepped across the marble hall, motioning his fingers to open the front door without touching the handle. It swung open.

"Kenneth Raibeart Aloysius MacGregor." His ma's hard voice reminded him of every time he'd been in trouble as a child. "Where do ya think ya are going with my granddaughter? Stop right there."

He wasn't given a choice but to obey. Magick hit his feet, petrifying his legs. He tried to move, but they were as frozen as stone.

"Ma, what—*och!*" The magick stopped blood flow through his legs and the pain was almost instant.

How did she know he was leaving?

Margareta rushed to pull the fully awake child from his arms before hitting the rest of his body with a petrifying spell. Jewel began to cry. "We'll talk about this later."

Chapter Three

Andrea stared at the needle hovering near empty in her old sedan and then at the motel. The place was the kind of roadside tarnished gem that often boasted cheap rooms and free cable. She'd stayed in places like this all over the United States and the rooms were always ugly and old. If she were lucky there wouldn't be bugs or strange smells.

"Car or room?"

It wouldn't be the first time she'd slept in her car. She tapped the side of her phone, thinking of her low bank balance. The action brought up her email.

We regret to inform you that we're dissolving the on-a-dime travel section. No more pieces will be acquired. Thank you for your past submissions.

"Car or room or food?" she whispered, trying to decide.

"*Badger!*"

Andrea jerked her attention to the parking lot in time to see a naked man streaking across the walkway in front of the long line of rooms. She lifted in her seat, attempting to see what was after him. Nothing came into view.

She let go of a surprised laugh as the naked ass disappeared down a corridor.

"Been there, buddy," she mumbled. Technically it was a lie. She'd never run naked through a motel parking lot being chased by an invisible badger.

Yet. The night was young. Anything was possible.

She wondered if she should make sure the man was all right.

Andrea reached for the door handle but lightning struck like a warning, only to be followed seconds later by an angry rumble of thunder. The 'H' on the motel sign flickered briefly before going out, followed by the 'L'. Her heart beat faster. A chill unfurled inside her chest. The threat of the storm made up her mind for her.

"Room. Vending machine." She grabbed a roll of quarters from the console and took out a few dollars' worth. "Sorry car. No gas for you until I find temporary work."

Storms had put her on edge ever since the swamp. Though it was unlikely danger lurked in the heavens this night, she still didn't want to be caught out in the middle of it.

Andrea grabbed the backpack with her laptop off the passenger seat. She slowly stepped out of her car, looking around for something that might have been chasing the naked guy. Not sensing any immediate danger, she hurried across the parking lot toward the motel lobby.

As the bell jingled over the door, she was greeted with a long check-in counter under a dim yellow light. The brown paneling on the walls and large wire rack display of local brochures were more or less what she'd expected. She scanned the offerings for leads on places to look for work—an Italian restaurant, a toiletry store called Love Potions, historic home tours, and a local tavern. An overgrown plant blocked a dark window. It sat next to a couch and an end table.

"Good evening." A man came through a door behind the check-in counter, wiping his hands on a paper towel. "I'm Fletch. How can I help you?"

He said the words without bothering to look at her.

"I need your cheapest room," Andrea answered.

Fletch glanced up and gave a small laugh. "All of our rooms are cheap."

"Perfect." Andrea lowered the backpack from her shoulder and rested it on the carpeted floor. "Any discount for late check-in?"

Fletch eyed her for a moment. "I think you qualify for the sixty-plus discount."

Andrea had turned thirty the week before. She touched her hair. The dark brown hair coloring hid the now-natural white.

"I noticed that some of the letters on your sign were flickering out," she said. "Why is the motel called Hotel?"

Fletch chuckled. "The owner tried to class this place up by changing its name from a motel to a hotel, but spent all his money on that sign, so he never got to the converting-us-to-a-hotel part of his plan. That sign has been flickering since the day they hoisted it up there."

Andrea hid her smile. Small towns always had their own bit of unique charm. "Also, you had a naked guy running through your parking lot. I don't know if he needed help or not."

"Really?" Fletch hurried around the counter to check the parking lot. "Where? I don't see him."

"He ran between a couple of the buildings," Andrea answered, following him as if by looking she could confirm what she already knew.

"Damn. The security cameras keep glitching. I wonder who it was." Fletch pushed the door open and stepped toward the cars and continued to search. A cool breeze stirred over her and it smelled like the moments before a rain.

Andrea had no idea who the naked man was so she simply shrugged when Fletch glanced at her for an answer.

"Did you see a kilt?" Fletch asked.

"As in Highlanders? No." Andrea stepped aside as the man came back into the lobby. "He was naked. All I saw was ass."

"Cute?"

Andrea laughed. "It didn't make me turn away if that's what you're asking."

"I'll bet it was one of the MacGregors." Fletch's tone instantly lowered into gossip mode.

Andrea was tired from a long day on the road but ended up prompting him anyway. "MacGregors?"

"They're this mysterious, wealthy family who just whisked into town one day and started buying all the property." He leaned forward, a smile curling the side of his mouth, as if this wasn't the first time he'd shared this bit of gossip with a newcomer. Seeing as he ran the front desk of a motel, she could see why. "And by family, I'm not talking mom, dad, and little Liam. I mean the whole family—aunts, uncles, cousins, sisters, brothers. You might as well rename Green Vallis into Little Scotland."

"So you think that's who was running naked through the parking lot? Eccentric millionaires?"

"Try billionaires." His voice lowered to a whisper. "All kinds of strange things have been happening since they arrived. They're hiding something big. I can tell. I have a nose for these things."

Andrea leaned closer to him as his voice dropped. A worried feeling knotted her stomach. Maybe it would be fuel and a vending machine tonight. "Strange how?"

"Lydia Barratt got married to one. Bagpipes and kilts on parade all through town for that proposal," Fletch said.

Andrea frowned, the anxious feeling going away. "A parade? That's what's weird?"

"No. Lydia getting married. She comes from a family of witches, you know, and even makes love potions. Literally. That's what her business is called, Love Potions. Some of the locals used to joke that she'd die a spinster like her aunt but the second billionaires roll into town she snags herself a husband."

"So you think this Lydia made a real love potion and then bespelled a man from the million —sorry *billion*—aire family?"

"Oh, no, Lydia is not nefarious or a gold digger type. I think they bespelled her," Fletch said.

Andrea gave what she hoped was an appropriately shocked expression, but really, she was over the conversation. This man was clearly just gossiping for the sake of spreading rumors. She'd bet money that if this guy saw a real supernatural witch, he'd pee himself. "Naked guys and witches? Thanks for the warning. I'll be sure to be careful."

"Or just have your camera ready." Fletch winked. He began what felt like an almost automated check-in procedure, pausing after each question for her answer as he typed it into his system. "Name? Number? Home Address? License plate number?"

Andrea had to lie about her address, otherwise she'd have to give her license plate twice.

"We don't have a buffet, but there will be coffee, donuts, and muffins here in the front office for breakfast. And that will be thirty-six dollars." He held his hand out.

Andrea gave him her bank card.

"If you decide to stay more than one night, I'll be on shift tomorrow afternoon." He winked at her, but she didn't get the impression he was flirting. Fletch's interests seemed to run toward the naked MacGregor man.

The website might not want cheap travel tips, but they'd probably pay for stories of sexy men in kilts. Too bad she wasn't that kind of journalist.

The wind had picked up as she hurried down the sidewalk toward her room, 124. The two was missing from the door but the impression it had left in the weathered paint was still there. As the metal key slid into the lock, she glanced over the parking lot toward her car to make a mental note of where it was located in relation to her room.

Andrea instantly locked the door and dropped her bag on the bed. Yellow flower designs stood out against the avocado green of the curtains. She drew them closed for privacy.

Out of habit, she went to her bag and pulled out a mason jar of red brick dust. She took a pinch and sprinkled it along the bottom of the door for protection. The large jar was a little less than a fourth full, so she wouldn't have to travel south too soon for more if she was conservative with her usage. It had come to the point she couldn't sleep without knowing she was shielded from the outside world. She put another pinch along the windowsill.

Andrea turned, studying the walls. At one time they had been cream, but the paper was browned and brittle. There was comfort to be found standing in a room, hidden away from the world outside. The brown carpet appeared as if it had been replaced within the last five years, the tightly wound pile worn in a path from the door, to the bed, to the bathroom, and less so to a chair and small desk.

Thunder rumbled outside.

Andrea took a deep breath. She was alone, safe.

"*Aahh.*"

Andrea tensed at the faint cry. It came from the direction of the bathroom. The door was cracked, but not enough to see inside.

Coldness crept inside her and, for a moment, she couldn't move. The cold came from a place of pure fear. It did not reason or relent. All she could do was protect herself against it.

Andrea should not have survived Mama Cecile. In many ways, she hadn't. That night marked her—each second since felt borrowed and filled with danger.

"*Wah-ah.*"

A baby? Here in the motel?

Her concern overrode her caution. She hurried into the bathroom, running her hand against the wall where the light switch should have been located. The child's cry became louder. The lights flickered and she blinked at the bright flash, automatically shading her eyes with a raised arm in an effort to see.

The sound stopped.

Even before Andrea lowered her arm, she knew something wasn't right.

A figure blocked her view and she gasped, jumping back, ready to defend herself. Her heart pounded and she took several deep breaths. The man didn't move. His limbs were frozen at a strange angle, as if he carried something that wasn't visible to the eye.

She found herself standing in a foyer with a marble floor and gaudy chandelier. Behind the man, a grand staircase led to a second story. She couldn't tell if this was a hotel or a home, but she knew this definitely wasn't the motel bathroom.

The male statue appeared lifelike. He wore jeans and a t-shirt. He seemed familiar, as if she'd met the model before but she couldn't place him. Aside from the strange arm positioning, he could have been anyone walking down the street. Since this was the only thing resembling human life, she crept forward and slowly touched his chest with the tip of her finger.

Heat radiated from him like he was a living being, but the ripples in the t-shirt material didn't move. The flat spot against the muscles of his chest showed that he'd once held an item. She thought to detect a heartbeat inside his chest. A living statue? How was that possible?

For some reason, she wanted to call him a prince, though he hardly looked like the fairytale version of royalty. Handsome as sin? Yes. Princely? No.

"Mister?" She tapped his arm, watching his face. "Can you hear me?"

His eyes moved and she jerked her hand away. He stared at her. When she'd spoken, she hadn't expected a response.

"Can I...?" She lightly touched his shoulder. His eyes darted toward her hand and then back to her face. "I'm sorry. I don't know what this is. I don't know how to help you."

Even though the skin around his eyes didn't move, she felt an urgency inside him. He stared at her, then to the right. She followed his gaze through a door to an empty dining room table.

She glanced around for a sign of why she'd been brought there. The front door was open.

Where there should have been a yard, she instead saw the wall of her motel room.

She glanced up at the man, wishing there was a way to free him but she didn't possess that kind of magick. This was surely born of dark intentions. Why else turn a man into a statue? She backed toward the door determined to run. "I'm sorry. I can't stay. I'll try to find—"

"Who are ya?" a woman's voice demanded. Her Scottish accent was thick. "What are ya doing in my home?"

Andrea ran into her motel room. The dizziness of passing through the invisible barrier caused her to weave on her feet. She glanced back to see a woman holding a baby. The image faded into black shadows.

She pressed her hand to her chest, breathing hard. "What the hell was that?"

Chapter Four

Andrea opened her eyes and stared at the ceiling in confusion. A ring stained the cheap fiber panels of the drop ceiling indicating there had been a water leak at one point.

"Where am I?" she whispered, trying to remember. Her mind was hazy, as if still coming from a deep sleep. Numbness radiated through her limbs. The coldness that she kept locked away in her chest tried to leak out. The nightmares had been bad this time, trapping her back in the swamp. When the dreams started, she never knew which version she would get—the one that ended with a hand in her chest, squeezing the life from her, or the one where an unseen force swept her away from danger and she felt safe.

Naturally, she preferred to feel safe. The fact

that the safety dream occasionally turned naughty where the rescuing force was a man with enough fire to fuel any single gal's sexual fantasies, well, that was just a bonus—a hot, fiery, much-welcome, ache-inducing bonus.

Last night, it had been the cold hand in her chest and the pain of a thousand deaths as the world ended in ashen chaos.

A drop of water leaked from a faucet some-where in the room.

Drip. Drip. Drip.

She turned toward the sound, seeing faded wallpaper and the ugly green floral print of the comforter she lay on.

Drip. Drip.

Thunder rumbled, and she looked to her left at the yellow and green curtains. Storms reminded her of Mama Cecile. No matter how much time passed, they always came back. Her days were borrowed. Death had already found her. It just needed to finish the job.

"Wisconsin." She was finally able to answer her own question. "At a motel called Hotel."

The words grounded her somewhat, drawing her from the lingering fear.

Her backpack rested close to her head, unzipped. Had she fallen onto the bed and gone instantly to sleep the second the brick dust was in place?

Andrea struggled to push herself up. She let her legs drop over the side of the bed and her shoes hit the carpet.

No. She wouldn't have gone to bed wearing her shoes.

The bathroom door wasn't visible from where she sat. What had happened didn't feel like a dream, and she knew better than to dismiss it as such.

Andrea took a deep breath to steady her nerves. No one was coming to help her. Whatever this was, she was on her own to deal with it.

She went to the bathroom door. It stood partially shut, just as she remembered seeing it before. The shadows from within parted to the light from the room as she pushed it open with her fingertips. It cast over a sink and toilet. She hesitated before reaching around the wall to feel for the light switch. She flipped it and jerked her hand out of the room. The bathroom remained.

Her first impulse was to jump in her car and leave. With the sad state of her bank account, that would be difficult. She wouldn't drive far on gas fumes and hope.

Andrea went to peek through the curtains. Morning light covered the parking lot. The skies were dark but the rain had stopped. There wasn't much of a view but her car was where she'd left it.

She zipped her backpack, placed it on the floor, and shoved the metal room key into her pocket. Fletch had mentioned there would be breakfast in the lobby. Andrea couldn't turn down free food.

She glanced down the sidewalk to check that it was empty before making her way toward the motel lobby. Mindful of the bells on the lobby door, she pulled it slowly to keep them from jingling too loudly. There was no reason to rouse the staff. As promised, a table had been laid out with a box of donuts, muffins in a plastic holder, and a coffee urn.

It had been over twenty-four hours since she'd had anything to eat and the hunger had moved past her empty stomach to her head. Her low blood sugar had manifested into dizziness.

Andrea waited to see if anyone would come to greet her through the door behind the desk. When they didn't, she grabbed the box and turned. Technically, it wasn't stealing. It just wasn't sharing with the other guests either.

She left as stealthily as she'd entered, jogging once she'd cleared the jingling door. Holding the box edge against her chest with one hand, she reached for the key with the other. She slipped inside her motel room and prayed no one saw her embarrassing donut heist.

Still holding the box, she turned to shut the door behind her, only to come face to face with a familiar woman. They stared at each other for a long moment.

The night before the lady had been holding a baby.

"Thank ya for coming." The woman glanced down at the threshold. She lifted her hand, gliding it over the doorway as if feeling the invisible barrier caused by the brick dust. "We've been expecting ya."

"I think you have the wrong room," Andrea said, knowing that the protection should keep any who meant her harm from crossing the threshold.

"Oh, ya shouldn't have." The woman reached inside and took the donut box of out Andrea's hands. "Very kind of ya to bring breakfast."

"I…" Andrea started to reach after the box. That was what she'd planned on eating all day.

"Grab your bag. I'll make coffee to go with these." The woman turned her back.

Andrea automatically glanced toward her backpack. The hotel room had disappeared and the bag now rested against the steps leading up to the front door. The motel was gone, replaced by a house. She took a step back, seeing the length of the exterior wall. This wasn't just a house. It was a mansion.

She looked down a hill. The motel was nowhere to be seen, though she still held the room key clutched in her fist. A town nestled in the valley below, accessible by a long stone driveway. There was a distant water tower, but it was too far away to read. Trees appeared to hug the sides of the home, though from her place, it was difficult to tell if it was a forest or just landscaping.

"Coming?"

Andrea shoved the key into her pocket and reached for her bag, realizing she had little choice but to play along. This could be the result of a portal in her motel room that wanted her at this mansion, or a past haunting that had her locked in its grasp as she lay on the hotel bed, unaware of where she was, or even a parallel world overlapping with her own that she'd accidentally stepped into.

Or, most terrifying of all, this was the curse that had been chasing her for two years.

Until Andrea knew what she was dealing with, she'd have to ride this strangeness out. It wasn't the first time she'd seen supernatural mysteries at play and spells this strong took cleverness to break.

She felt her nose burn as tears threatened, not out of fear this time but from frustration. All she wanted was a normal life. She'd jumped in her car and ran to find it. And here she was, in Nowhere, Wisconsin, facing down a mysterious power.

If this was indeed still Wisconsin.

She stared through the front door at the foyer. The statue of the man was gone, but the stairs were the same.

The woman reemerged from within and arched a brow. "Well, then, come on."

"How…?" Andrea whispered, again glancing around in hopes that the motel would reappear. For the time being she could see no way back to her room. "How may I help you?"

"That's what we're here to talk about, isn't it?" The woman laughed.

Andrea forced her feet to step across the threshold. The woman led the way out of the foyer. If she were lucky, whatever this was would end soon and she'd be back at the motel.

"Hey, Ma, I have to go pick up Uncle Raibeart." A man's voice came from the same direction the woman had gone. "Cora found him passed out in the mass market paperback section of the library."

"Not again," the woman answered. "Bring an extra coat with ya. We don't want him scaring the locals."

Andrea peeked into the dining room. A man

stopped his progress toward her and gave her an easy smile. "Oh, hello. I didn't realize we had company."

He wasn't the same person she'd seen frozen in the foyer but looked as if he could have been related.

"I'm Euann MacGregor."

"Andrea," she answered, not taking the hand he offered.

"Pleasure to meet ya." He moved past her, forcing her to step aside. "Excuse me. I'm expected downtown."

Euann's footsteps moved toward the front door.

Andrea studied her surroundings. The woman must have gone through the dining room to another part of the house. Seeing the box of donuts on the table, she hurried to pull out a glazed and stuffed it into her mouth, eating as fast as she could. She was in the process of grabbing a second helping when the woman reappeared in the dining room carrying a silver serving set. On it were two white mugs, sugar cubes, and creamer.

Andrea dropped a chocolate cake donut back into the box and closed the lid. Already she was beginning to feel better with food in her stomach.

"You're younger than I'd thought you'd be."

The woman set the tray on the shiny wood tabletop.

"Who are you?" Andrea asked, wondering why the woman had thought about her at all.

"Margareta MacGregor." She began pouring coffee into the mugs.

Andrea had already guessed by the accent that they were the mysterious family Fletch had gossiped about that had been buying up all the property in Green Vallis. At least that meant she was probably still in the same town.

"What am I doing here, Margareta MacGregor?"

"I assume you're here about the job, Andrea." Margareta gestured toward the serving set. "Cream? Sugar?"

"Black." Andrea frowned. "How do you know my name?"

"Ya told my son, Euann." Margareta smiled as she placed a mug on the table, as if unconcerned about the polished top. "Doesn't take a psychic to eavesdrop."

"Is that what you are? A psychic?" Andrea couldn't help but wonder what had happened to the statue man. What kind of magick was at work here? "Is that why you were expecting me?"

"The way ya say that," Margareta said, her

accented voice soft, "it wouldn't surprise ya if I told ya I am."

"There are things in this world that cannot be explained with logic and science." Andrea found no reason for pretense. The sooner she figured out what they wanted, the sooner she'd be on her way. Her eyes strayed to the donut box, wishing she'd been given another minute alone with it.

"You're talking about magick." Margareta came around to the head of the table to stand closer. "The old ways."

"I'm talking about the portal you created in my motel bathroom last night, and then again in my doorway." Andrea leaned away, not wanting to stand too close to a magickal being.

"Portal? Motel?" The woman glanced around the room, confused. "Ya came to my house this morning."

Shit.

If Margareta didn't know what was going on either…

Shit. Shit. Shit.

Had she caused this? Andrea had never summoned such magick before.

What was going on in this town? Maybe she shouldn't have dismissed Fletch so quickly when he said strange things happened here.

"Ignore me. Bad joke. I'm told I have an odd

sense of humor. Yes. I'm here looking for a job." Andrea knew it was a lame cover after she'd talked about portals and psychics.

"Do ya have experience with children?" Margareta asked.

Andrea shook her head in denial. "No."

"But ya want to be a nanny to my granddaughter?"

A what? Andrea stiffened. She'd just assumed the job would be something like housekeeping or helping at one of the many properties this family owned in town.

"I... guess," Andrea answered. Either Margareta had given birth at a very young age, or genetics had blessed this family with a youthful gene. "Are you just looking for someone to take her to school and ballet or soccer practice?"

"Jewel is two years old." Margareta smiled, her eyes staying focused on Andrea's face.

Crap. Of course. She'd also seen Margareta holding an infant the night before.

"And would this be for the infant as well?" Andrea asked.

"I only have one grandchild," Margareta said. "Jewel is the only baby in this house."

"Oh." There were times when conversations just flowed naturally and easily. This was not one of them. Every word between them felt labored.

None of this made sense. She might not know much about child development, but she knew the difference between an infant and a toddler.

Andrea tried to think of what to say next, but all she could come up with was, "I don't know anything about two-year-olds."

"I see." Margareta nodded once. "Then perhaps you're not the best person for the—"

The sound of a crying child erupted from another room.

"That doesn't sound right." Margareta frowned. She hurried through the dining room.

Andrea followed the woman past a kitchen to what looked like a combination library and home office. A child lay on a blanket in the middle of the floor, her limbs twitching. She was dressed in pink pajamas with cartoon bulldogs on them.

"Should I call an ambulance?" Andrea hadn't lied when she said she didn't know anything about children. She liked them, but she didn't have any experience with things like this. At most, she gave them cookies during family reunions and guiltily sent them back to their parents filled with sugar.

"For a tantrum?" Margareta dismissed, kneeling by Jewel. She stroked the child's hair. "What are ya doing down here, wee one?"

Andrea wasn't sure what to do. She stood in

the doorway, wondering if she should help or leave.

"Can ya hand me the diaper bag?" Margareta asked.

Andrea retrieved the yellow diaper bag from the oak desk. As she handed it to the woman, the child's hand smacked her foot.

The crying instantly stopped.

She felt movement against her shoe and looked down. Jewel stared up at her, babbling incoherent toddler words as she played with Andrea's shoestrings.

"You're hired," Margareta said.

Andrea frowned. "What?"

"My son is a single father and he needs help. As much as I'd enjoy having this little lovebug with me, the MacGregor family businesses are not always conducive to having a toddler at my side."

"Euann?"

"Kenneth" Margareta answered. "He's my fourth out of six. He's housebound. Children need light, and air, and socialization outside of the family. That is what you'll provide."

"Does he work for the MacGregor family businesses as well?" Andrea asked, staring at the little hand touching her foot. She wasn't paying much attention to what she was saying. Something about the child mesmerized her.

"All my children work for the family businesses."

"Do they all live locally?"

Margareta reached for a chair to pull herself to standing. "Erik, my oldest, lives just down the hill with his wife, Lydia. Euann stays here with his wife, Cora. Iain lives with his wife, Jane. They have a place near her garden nursery here in town. My only daughter, Malina, is in Las Vegas with her husband, Dar. And Niall, my baby, is nomadic. He travels with his wife, Charlotte. I do miss the days they were all under one roof, but I suppose children must eventually marry. Now I'm hoping for more grandchildren."

"Her eyes are like wine, I drink them with mine," a man sang, the words loud and slurred. "My sweet lassie bride, as beautiful as the day we met."

Margareta sighed and gave a wry shake of her head. "And that off-key buffoon would be my husband."

The buffoon in question charged through the door with his arms spread wide. Mud caked his kilt and naked chest. "So loving and forgiving, she—"

"Angus MacGregor—" Margareta started to scold.

"There's my sweet rose," Angus interrupted,

grinning at his wife as if he could charm his way out of being in trouble.

"Did ya lose something last night?" Margareta demanded.

"My heart to my beautiful wife?" Angus grinned.

"Try again," Margareta said.

Angus patted his hips and then his naked chest as if checking pockets that weren't there.

"Your brothers?" Margareta prompted.

"Oh, right, them." Angus glanced the way he'd come before saying. "I've come to fetch clothes for Murdoch. Don't tell Cait. Let her enjoy her trip. It wasn't our fault this time." His eyes landed on Andrea. "Who do we have here?"

"Andrea Breaux," Andrea answered.

"Jewel's new nanny," Margareta added.

"If you're trying to find him, I think I saw your naked brother at the motel last night, running through the corridors," Andrea offered. "He was being chased by a badger, I think? Though I didn't see it."

Angus gave a sheepish grin. "Wrong naked brother."

"Euann is picking Raibeart up from the library," Margareta said. "You're lucky Cora was there to find him."

Angus laughed. "Cora always opens the

library. He wasn't in any danger. We told him one of his old girlfriends wrote a book about him and sent him to the romance section. Kept him busy for the night."

Andrea ducked her head and bit back a laugh. Angus appeared so earnest, and Margareta so filled with wifely exasperation.

"A romance novel." Margareta shook her head. "Like a woman would write a book about any of ya fools."

"Kept him out of trouble, didn't it?" Angus chuckled. He tried to hug his wife. "And I know ya would write a book about me if only ya could put your great love into words."

"Get cleaned up." Margareta swatted him in dismissal. "We'll discuss this later."

Andrea watched him leave. They seemed like a nice family but she didn't want to be anywhere near this place. She wanted to be in her car, speeding away.

Margareta smiled. "I have a good feeling about this."

Jewel looked like a sweet kid, but that didn't change facts. "I'm sorry, I can't accept the position."

"It pays five-fifty a week," Margareta said.

"I…" Andrea shook her head. She needed the money, but…

"And lodging."

"I…"

"Jewel likes ya," Margareta continued. "If it doesn't work out, ya can always give your notice."

"I…" Andrea took a deep breath, letting it out slowly. She thought of her car. The tank was empty and she needed tires and an oil change. She thought of the motel. It would be nice to stay in a place that didn't smell like decay. And then she thought of the donuts. It would be amazing to actually afford a meal without first checking her bank account or having to sneak it out of a motel lobby.

Circumstances made it impossible to say no. She needed a job, and this one had fallen into her lap, or rather, invaded her motel room. Margareta didn't appear to notice the portals, so there was a chance the woman had no clue of the magick going on around her. If that was true, this family needed her help. Could she walk away from this?

Andrea opened her mouth to answer but only managed a faint nod.

"Wonderful!" Margareta gave a small clap of her hands. "That's settled."

"Ma, have ya seen Jewel?" The sound of panic came from the direction of the front hall.

"She's in here, Kenneth," Margareta called out to her son.

"She kicked off her bracelets again." The man who'd been frozen like a statue appeared in the doorway. He held two pieces of bent metal.

Relief filled her to see the man was no longer trapped. She studied his face, wondering if he recognized her.

"Kenneth, meet your new nanny, Andrea," Margareta said.

Andrea lifted her hand in a small wave. She wondered what was wrong with Kenneth that made him housebound. He appeared healthy—now that he could move.

Kenneth looked as if he was trying to remember where he'd seen her before. He arched a brow at her before saying wryly, "I think I'm a little too old for a nanny."

"For your…" Andrea motioned to the child on the floor.

He gave a small laugh. "That was a joke."

"Of course." Andrea peered at the child. Jewel seemed content to play with her foot. Did they expect her to do something?

"I should get back to the motel," Andrea said. Hopefully the map app on her phone could show her the way if a portal to her room didn't appear.

Crap. Where was her phone?

Kenneth leaned over and slipped two bent metal bracelets onto Jewel's ankles before lifting the child from the floor. "Thank ya for coming to interview, but ya have been misinformed. We don't need—"

"A motel room for ya," Margareta broke in, though it was clear her son was about to undo her hire. "Of course ya will stay here. That only makes sense. Ya will take Malina's room. She's not using it."

"We don't need a nanny," Kenneth repeated. "I can take care of my daughter."

Jewel began to cry.

Margareta reached for the child, taking her out of Kenneth's arms before handing her to Andrea.

"Oh!" Andrea caught the toddler against her chest in surprise. The child instantly stopped crying and smiled. Fingers wound into Andrea's hair as Jewel started jabbering a long stream of toddler words as if trying to impart a very important message.

"It's settled," Margareta stated. "Jewel likes her."

Kenneth frowned.

"I'll call the motel and arrange to have any outstanding bills settled. Do ya have luggage we need to have brought to the house?"

"Just my car. It's in the motel parking lot," Andrea said.

"I'll send Rory for it." Margareta started to leave the room.

"Wait." Andrea adjusted the child onto her hip then dug into her pocket to pull out the key. "Here's my room key."

Margareta came back, took the key, and then left again.

"My car keys should be on the nightstand," Andrea called after the woman.

Andrea hesitated before glancing up at Kenneth. He openly stared at her, not seeming pleased that she held his daughter.

"I understand if you would like someone more qualified to help with Jewel," Andrea said. "She's your daughter. Just say the word and I'll—*ow!*"

Jewel yanked her hair hard.

"Have we met before today?"

"Not officially," Andrea said, not wanting to bring up abandoning him while he was a statue. "I'm Andrea Breaux."

"How did ya find out about this job?" He didn't attempt to help her untangle Jewel's fingers. "If ya are at the motel, ya clearly do not live in the area."

Between Margareta, Angus, Kenneth, and the toddler yanking on her hair, this had to be the strangest job interview.

"I arrived in town last night," she said.

50

"Where do ya live?" he asked, the words guarded, as if he expected her to give him a reason to kick her out. It was too bad. She had the impression that the man could have easily been charming if he just bothered to smile.

"From all over." All she could do was answer honestly. "I was a travel writer."

"Was?"

"My position was cut."

"And so ya thought you'd drive here and become a nanny?" His tone felt accusatory, though she wasn't sure what he accused her of doing.

"I stopped for the night and found out about the position this morning." Andrea adjusted Jewel to her other hip and leaned to support the wiggling child's weight.

"That seems very coincidental."

"If you say so."

"Why do ya want this job?"

"I need to work."

"Why?"

"I need money."

"Is that all?"

Andrea felt her irritation growing. This man clearly didn't want her there. Why was she even bothering?

"Essentially," she said. "Money pays for

motels, gas, food… all things I'm rather fond of being able to afford. I don't expect a man like you, with all this wealth, to understand what it is like to be broke, to have to decide if I want to put gas in the car or have a safe place to sleep for the night because I can't do both, and I don't like camping in my car during thunderstorms. I'll bet you have never had to charm the guy at the front desk into giving you a room discount. Or had to steal a box of free-for-guests donuts from a motel lobby because the bruised, discount-bin-gas-station apple I had for lunch the day before wasn't doing the trick, and I was lightheaded, and if I spread them out, the donuts could last me a couple of days. So yes. I want any job I can find. I want the job as a nanny. I'm a good person. I'd never hurt a child and Jewel likes me. But if you aren't going to hire me, then I need to keep looking."

Andrea tried to hand the child to her father. Jewel kicked her feet. The metal bracelets slipped off her ankles. A bright light flashed and Kenneth disappeared, as did the office.

Andrea drew the child back to her chest as she slowly turned to examine their new surroundings. This time there hadn't been a doorway to pass through. Soft pinks and blues instantly gave away the fact this was a child's room. A strange mix of ballerinas and toy soldiers littered the floor, as if the dolls had been at the same playtime party. A table with a tea set was pushed into a corner. Books lined a long shelf opposite a crib.

The toddler laughed and kicked her feet. Andrea slowly set her down on the floor by her toys. Jewel's green eyes flashed with what looked to be flames.

The soldiers and ballerinas stood up from the floor and began moving, their plastic limbs stiff as they walked around the child.

"Da da swilly," Jewel declared before laughing.

Andrea backed away from the girl. What kind of magick was this? Flames in the eyes? Surely that had to be some kind of demonic presence at work. She'd only seen that sort of thing once before.

Mama Cecile's eyes had lit with fire.

Andrea darted for the bedroom door, throwing it open and running through, only to find herself back in the child's room. Andrea turned to try again, but she saw Jewel and her moving toys through the doorway. The child was also behind her. There was no escape.

Seeing another door, she rushed across the room. Inside was a bathroom. A blue bathmat laid on the black-and-white tile floor. Two imprints of adult knees flattened it as if someone had spent time kneeling before the tub. Toys rested at the bottom of the bath. There was no way out besides the doorway she'd come through.

Water began filling the tub without anyone touching it. Suddenly a splash sounded, and Jewel appeared sitting in the water. She still wore her clothes, laughing and giggling. Her hands slapped the surface and her legs kicked. The motion sent her bottom sliding.

On reflex, Andrea lurched forward and caught the toddler before she fell over.

"Bat," Jewel said, squealing.

Andrea reached to turn the faucet off before the water became too deep.

"Jewel?" Kenneth's voice sounded panicked.

"Here," Andrea called, awkwardly leaning over the tub.

Kenneth appeared in the doorway, breathing hard. His eyes went from Andrea to the child and then back again. "I can explain."

"I don't need to know." Andrea made sure the child was balanced before letting go. "I didn't see anything. I just want to go now. Please let me out."

"It's not me. It's…" He looked at Jewel. "She likes ya."

He held the bent metal bands, angling his hand as if to hide them from the child's view.

Andrea backed out of his way as he went to his daughter. He knelt on the bathmat and gently stroked the girl's hair. His voice softened. "There ya are, naughty lassie."

"Bat!" Jewel splashed her hands and giggled.

"It's not time for your bath," Kenneth disagreed.

Andrea left the bathroom and again tried the door to the nursery. It was like looking into a mirror that held everything but her reflection.

"She's not dangerous." Kenneth appeared beyond the door holding Jewel swaddled in a towel, but his voice came from behind. The optical illusion was messing with her senses and she turned to face him.

"I won't tell anyone. No one would believe it. I just want to get back on the road." Andrea watched the child's eyes for changes.

"I thought ya needed work," he countered.

"I thought you said you didn't want a nanny."

"Jewel likes ya." Kenneth bounced the child on his hip.

"Jewel is a toddler. I'm not sure she's equipped to make childcare decisions." Andrea glanced at the toys on the floor. They no longer moved on their own.

I can't help a toddler possessed by a demon. I faced darkness before and I failed.

Jewel's eyes filled with flames. One moment she was in her father's arms in soggy clothes and a towel, and the next she stood in a pink tutu and green leotard.

"Where is that wee bairn? Ya better not have started without your uncle Raibeart."

Andrea spun around just in time to step out of the man's way.

Jewel giggled, and said, "Beart."

Raibeart stopped short of running into her.

Andrea recognized the man, even though he wore a kilt and black t-shirt. "Hey, you're the naked guy from the motel."

"I need to get a better nickname." Raibeart laughed. "Did I propose to ya, lassie? Are ya here to marry me?"

"Um, no." Andrea shook her head.

"Don't look so sad. I'm sure I will soon." Raibeart patted her on the arm. "I don't mean to break hearts. It's just a consequence of being so desirable."

Andrea arched a brow and gave him a bemused look.

"Ah, there's my little princess." Raibeart knelt on the floor next to the child. He waved his hand at Kenneth. "Off with ya. This is a private tea party." He went to lift the small table from the corner and carry it into the middle of the room.

Andrea glanced at the door. She saw the hallway and hurried through. One direction ended with a door, the other opened up with a handrail and daylight. She raced toward the rail, which brought her to the staircase leading to the front door.

"Andrea, wait," Kenneth called behind her.

Andrea ran faster, stumbling to get down the steps before the sweet demonic child stopped her again.

"Please," Kenneth pleaded.

She reached the front door and pulled it open. A cool breeze hit her.

"Please." The word was softer this time. "Stop. I can't follow ya outside."

Andrea turned to face him as he came down the steps. "I won't tell what I saw, but I can't be here."

"My daughter is," he looked upward toward Jewel's room, "special."

"I think you might have better luck with a priest or a shaman, anyone who can perform an exorcism," Andrea said.

Kenneth's eyes whipped around to meet hers. "Ya think she's possessed?"

"I saw the fire in her. What else could it be?"

"Jewel is not a demon," Kenneth protested, seeming offended by the idea.

"Her eyes had flames in them," Andrea countered. "I'm sorry, but that doesn't sound like any other kind of paranormal event. Regardless, I can't help you. I have my own demons to deal with."

"She's not demonic, she's…" Kenneth ran his hand through his hair. "She's magickal and she's in the terrible twos. She's been a handful lately, especially since she figured out how to get out of her binding bracelets."

Andrea heard the sound of a car coming up the drive.

"But she's never harmed anyone," he continued. "At worst, she makes them do whatever she wants. For a two-year-old, that's usually dress-up, story time, or sneaking cookies."

"My answer is no." Andrea saw a man pulling her vehicle to park alongside the drive and realized her backpack was missing. Her desire to get out of the house caused her to move quickly. She rushed through the dining room to the office library.

Her backpack was tipped over on the floor as if it dropped when Jewel made them disappear. The contents that had been in the side pockets had spilled onto the floor. Andrea knelt to repack her belongings, shoving them unceremoniously inside.

"I wish you luck finding a nanny who can help, Mr. MacGregor, but I have to go."

Chapter Five

Kenneth watched the frantic woman scurrying to get out of the MacGregor home. Just as Andrea put the last of her belongings in her bag and tried to stand, the zipper came undone and a laptop, along with several other items, slid out.

"Dammit," she swore, again starting the task of packing to leave.

Kenneth hadn't dated since before he'd met Jewel's mother. There wasn't room in his life for anything more than a one-night stand, and those were very few and far between. Still, he'd have to be braindead not to notice the beautiful woman in front of him. Dark curls were pulled to the nape of her neck but several had sprung free to frame her face. Her stylish dark shirt draped her body, clinging as she moved. He found himself mesmer-ized by the teasing curves.

Her dark eyes were guarded and watchful, but he didn't detect any malice in them. If anything, she was terrified. Could he blame her? She wasn't the first human to be caught up in Jewel's magick. In her last life, his daughter had kidnapped a woman and magickally compelled her to drive halfway across country to Wisconsin. It wasn't a stretch to think Jewel compelled a person she liked to be her nanny.

Kenneth didn't want to be the one to tell Andrea if it wasn't an unpacking bag, it would be something else. Once Jewel's magick made up its mind, it was difficult to stop. Even if Raibeart kept Jewel in the binding bracelets, the enchant-ment on Andrea's backpack was already set.

Seeing a mason jar rolling toward his foot, he picked it up. Andrea's eyes widened as he held it and she stared up at him.

Kenneth shook the red dust, feeling the power trapped inside.

"Tea," Andrea lied, lifting her hand. "It relaxes me and helps me sleep."

Kenneth suppressed his bemusement. "How about I make ya a cup now?"

"Oh, no," she shook her head. "That won't be necessary. I need to get on the road. I…"

"Don't want to drink brick dust to prove you're not lying?" he finished when her words trailed off.

"You know what it is?" Andrea stood, keeping her hand extended. He nodded. "Do you know what it's for?"

Kenneth glanced at the floor, seeing a packet of rusted nails, a few vials, a box of dark hair color, and charms. He handed her the jar. "Folk magick."

Andrea shoved the jar into her bag along with the other contents and closed it. She made a fist around the zipper, holding tight, before lifting it from the floor. The second she took a step for the office door, the bottom of the bag busted, dropping all of the contents at her feet.

Kenneth flinched.

Andrea stared at the floor for a long time—so long in fact that he almost asked her if she was all right.

"I guess I'm staying." The flatness of her tone sounded resigned to the inevitable. "But I want double what your mother promised."

"Done," he answered without hesitation. His family could well afford to pay her a hundred times that.

"And I want you to tell me what's wrong with

your daughter. I can't help if I don't know what we're up against."

Kenneth stiffened. There was nothing *wrong* with his daughter. "How much do ya know about magick?"

"More than I want," Andrea answered.

"How deep does your folk magick go?" He felt like they both had secrets they were unwilling to share. His family had stringent rules when it came to talking about magick to humans. Well, in reality, there was only one rule pertaining to humans: Don't let them find out.

"Generations."

Her answer revealed very little.

The MacGregors' survival depended on secrecy, but it wasn't just about the warlocks. It was about all supernatural creatures. History had portrayed everyone who wasn't pure human as evil monsters. Humans feared supernaturals and saw them as a threat. It didn't take a genius to figure out what happened next. Shifters had been hunted to near extinction. Witches and warlocks had been burned at the stake, along with some unlucky non-magicks caught up in the sweeps. Vampires were staked in their sleep. Fairy rings were destroyed. Nymph playgrounds were burned to the ground.

The horrors had seemed endless.

Not to say that all supernatural creatures were innocent. Some deserved their fates. Darkness roamed the world, looking for ways to spread it's evil, sometimes it was human, and sometimes it was supernatural. That darkness wanted to exploit his daughter's powers.

The lure to use unharnessed magick was tempting, like a drug, but everything came with a cost. Even the MacGregors struggled with it. In order to fuel his powers, he had to take from something else. He could kill acres of forest in one evening if he wanted to, stealing life from nature and turning it to magick. It would feel amazing and be terribly wrong.

So which was Andrea? He wanted to believe she was good, but just because he wanted something didn't make it real.

When he merely studied her, trying to decide how much to tell her, she finally said. "I know enough about magick to know the items in my," she glanced to the mess on the floor and amended, "the items at my feet are not merely cute superstitions. Whatever thrall this family is under, I can try to help, but I'm not making any promises."

If she stayed willingly that was better than by force. It's not like he could kick her out if he wanted to. Jewel would keep bringing her back. At least this way he could keep an eye on her as he figured out her intentions.

"Coming through!" Raibeart yelled as he ran past in a green leotard and yellow tutu. "That girl of yours is a playful thing, but she's too young to put the hot stuff in my tea party juice."

Kenneth leaned out of the way as his uncle went to the liquor cabinet. Andrea's eyes widened as she stared at the man in the ridiculous outfit.

"Thank ya for not making my two-year-old daughter serve ya whiskey," Kenneth said.

"Your aunt Cait threatened me," Raibeart answered, grabbing a bottle and grinning as he looked at it in appreciation.

"Is Cait your wife?" Andrea asked.

"I don't think I'm married." Raibeart appeared confused by the question.

"Aunt Cait is married to Murdoch," Kenneth answered for his uncle as Raibeart did a little pirouette with the bottle.

"That's right. Angus said as much." Andrea nodded.

Raibeart danced his way from the office. Though athletic, it was evident he didn't have ballet training.

"So…" Andrea pointed after the man. "Is he…?"

"No. Believe it or not, he's not under any spell." Kenneth gave a wry laugh.

"Should we be worried?" Andrea slowly moved to look out the door after Raibeart. In doing so, she came closer to Kenneth's chest. The scent of her light perfume hit him like a fireball to the gut. His magick automatically tried to draw energy from her.

For a warlock, two things could fuel their magick—nature and sex. It's why they lived by so many acres. They could take a little from each tree without killing any one plant. Sex was more like an explosion of energy created from the friction of two joining bodies.

He really, *really* wanted that explosion right now.

He looked at her ass, unable to stop himself.

Her weight shifted and his eyes darted back up. She furrowed a brow, having caught him.

"Raibeart won't hurt Jewel," Kenneth said, not giving her time to comment on his inappropriate behavior. Dragging her off to his bedroom probably wasn't the best way to calm her fears about being trapped in the mansion.

At least, not yet.

Maybe…

No. He needed to stop thinking about those things. There was no room in his life for such complications. The only reason he was feeling this way had to be because he was confined to the mansion. It's not like he had much contact with single women while housebound.

"Is everything all right?" Andrea slowly backed away from him. She stared at his face.

"Why wouldn't it be?"

"You're mumbling and making faces," Andrea said. "Would you like me to make you a cup of tea? Or should I get someone?"

"I don't drink brick dust." He was trying to make a joke, but it was lost on her.

"Maybe you could tell me where I'll be staying." Andrea leaned over to gather several of the spilled items off the floor—the ones used for protection and the hair color. He looked closer at her hair detecting a hint of white new growth behind her ear. "Kenneth?"

"Oh, um," he glanced down to where most of the elders slept in a wing beyond the dining room and library, before gesturing toward the front hall, "you'll have a room and private bathroom upstairs."

She motioned that he should lead the way. Kenneth gathered the rest of her belongings on top of the bag and cradled them against his chest to carry them.

"Hello? Is anyone here?" Rory, his cousin, called from the front hall.

"What is this place?" Andrea whispered to herself. "Grand Central Station?"

"My cousin Rory," Kenneth answered. "He lives here, too."

"Of course he does," she said under her breath.

"I have car keys. At least, I hope it's the right car." Rory stood in the front hall jingling a set of keys. He dropped his hand when he saw Kenneth. Then, as his eyes went to Andrea, he grinned. "Well, hello, beautiful."

Andrea smiled at the man.

"Don't," Kenneth warned, not liking the idea of his cousin flirting with Andrea. His body was still tight with need and the sudden surge of jealousy that filled him was unexpected.

The family resemblance ran strong in the MacGregor family. Rory had been blessed with the MacGregor green eyes. The color was prevalent in the family, though a few of Kenneth's siblings had brown. The man's brown hair had been tipped artificially with blond. His dandy of a cousin spent a little too much time at the salon.

"Ya were empty. I filled your gas tank," Rory said, somehow managing to make the words sound dirty.

"Thank you." Andrea reached to take the keys. "I'll pay you back as soon as I get—"

"Pay me back?" Rory laughed. "Don't worry about it, love. How about ya come to dinner with me tonight instead?"

"Oh, I—"

"She's working tonight," Kenneth interrupted. "I need her help with Jewel."

"Can't ya do it? It's not like you're going anywhere," Rory dismissed.

"He's right. I don't want to start a new job by asking for day one off," Andrea said.

"Perhaps a rain check, then." Rory finally dropped the keys in her hand. "The nachos at the Crimson Tavern are life changing." Then, turning to Kenneth, he added, "Not that ya would know anything about that, being as you're on house arrest. Isn't that right, Ken? Ya been a naughty boy, haven't ya?"

Rory slapped Kenneth on the arm hard before strolling toward the dining room.

"Oh, donuts. Nice," Rory said to no one in particular. "Don't mind if I do."

Kenneth motioned for Andrea to go upstairs but she wasn't paying attention. Her eyes were trained on the dining room door.

"He was joking. I'm not under arrest," Kenneth said, thinking the comment had to have worried her. "I don't want ya to be frightened by me. I'm not a criminal."

"What? Oh, no, I was just thinking…" She waved her hand in dismissal. "Donuts. It's nothing."

It was a weak coverup. Who worried about donuts? Kenneth decided to let the matter drop though he might have a few words with his dumbass cousin later.

"Ma said ya could take Malina's room. It's stocked for a woman and my sister won't be back anytime soon. She lives in Vegas with her husband," Kenneth said. His sister was married to a luck demon, and for Dar there was no better place than Las Vegas to feed on good and bad fortunes.

"If you're sure she won't mind," Andrea said.

"Not at all. Help yourself to whatever ya find. My brother Erik's wife owns Love Potions here in town," he said. "Malina's room is stocked with the stuff."

"I don't mess with potions." Andrea stopped on her way up the stairs. "I'm telling you now that I don't approve of taking a person's will away from them."

"Love Potions is the name of her bath and body shop," Kenneth explained. "Lydia makes shampoos and other girly stuff. Apparently, it's very popular on the internet."

"I wouldn't know. I don't shop online," Andrea answered. "But I think I saw a brochure for it at the hotel last night."

"If ya don't like what's in there, we can always order something else," he said.

"I'm sure it will be fine. I'm not picky." Andrea gripped the railing, pulling as if she needed to force herself to take each step. She cradled the mason jar, charms, and hair color against her chest. "Do I have time to shower, or do you need me to get started right away?"

"Please, settle in," he said. "No need to rush. Raibeart will keep Jewel entertained for hours if we let him."

Chapter Six

Andrea sat in the middle of the large bed, her legs crossed, as she rubbed her temples. Her hair was damp from the shower. The smell of rosemary lingered in her hair and on her skin. Kenneth had undersold the number of product options in his sister's bathroom. The woman had a floor-to-ceiling shelf lined with bottles. She also had a closet full of designer clothes. Andrea found a clean t-shirt and pair of sweatpants, choosing not to play dress-up in the more expensive choices.

Since a pinch of brick dust hadn't been enough to protect her in the motel room, she'd poured a line in front of the bedroom door and along the windows. She'd tried to conserve it, but there wasn't much left now. It looked as if her next stop would have to be Louisiana to restock. The idea of going back left her shaking.

Had this been three years ago, she would have been excited to stay in such a beautiful mansion bedroom. It was the kind of luxury only seen in movies. Dark wood accented the lighter walls. Nothing looked cheap or fake. A painting hung over a fireplace, the Impressionist landscape nothing but splotches of color creating what appeared to be a castle on a hillside.

She'd sprinkled brick dust in front of the fireplace as well. It was barren, but she didn't want to risk anything slipping in from outside. She'd hung coin-size charms in the windows and another from the fireplace mantel. Her grandmother would have said it was overkill. Her grandmother's cousin would have said it wasn't enough.

It didn't feel like enough to Andrea.

Andrea began to rock on the bed. Was this the start of the vision from Mama Cecile that she'd been running from? Jewel had the same fire in her eyes. Is this how the world ended? At the hands of a playful toddler?

Andrea didn't want to be here.

She couldn't leave.

Something deep inside told her she was where she needed to be. That didn't change the fact she wanted to run. If she stayed in one place for too long the spirit chasing her always returned to send her packing. Moving from place to place was the only way to stay safe.

Andrea stood from the bed and crossed the floor barefoot. From the window, she saw the gentle slope of the hill leading to town. A giant oak tree stood proud in the expansive lawn, apart from the smaller trees lining the cobblestone driveway. Several cars had been parked along the edge. They had not been there earlier, each of them fancy compared to her weather-beaten sedan.

The sound of 1920s jazz music came from within the home, the rhythm muffled by the closed door. It reminded her of her grandmother's house when she was little. The music drew her toward the bedroom door, filling her with the memory of being small. The children were often sent to bed before the adults' party started but she could always hear the shouts of laughter rising above the songs. There was comfort in the sound.

She pushed the door open. The music became louder. Andrea closed her eyes, listening for the laughter.

"We can't wait and see," a memory whispered. "We have to do it now. The signs have never been so clear. It's tonight."

Andrea didn't recognize the voice but her

imagination was convinced the words had been said.

When she opened her eyes, the dimly lit hall leading to her grandmother's living room and kitchen stretched beyond the MacGregor doorframe. A light came from where the kitchen would be, spilling over into the hall at a sharp angle.

Another portal? To the past?

Andrea was tempted to jump the barrier into her childhood where it had been safe.

"She needs our help." The voice was clearer than her memory had been, coming from beyond the door.

"Grandmama Ruth?" Andrea whispered.

"You heard what the spirits said." Aunt Florence wasn't technically Andrea's aunt but she was her grandmother's cousin, and that's what all of the kids called her. In her grandparents' generation, living in the Deep South, people had questioned why a black woman and a white woman would so openly acknowledge being first cousins, as if that family secret was something they should have denied. At least, that's the undertone Andrea always heard in the stories. To their credit, they never acted ashamed of their connection.

Andrea was raised believing in the bonds of family. And there were times she could have easily lied about who they were. Telling people you believed in folk magick wasn't exactly an easy way to grow up.

"She's just a child," Ruth argued. "There is still time."

"It won't be pleasant, but life rarely is," Florence said. "Either you do it or I will."

The sounds became hushed whispers, as if the two women walked farther away to argue beneath the peppier music.

A shadow moved past the kitchen doorway moments before her grandmother appeared in the hall. Her naturally graying hair was colored a stark black. Florence used to tease Ruth about trying too hard to resist nature.

"*Time marches across us all, cher. Eventually, it's gonna leave tracks,*" Florence had said more times than Andrea could count.

Ruth wore a simple dress and carried a champagne glass between two fingers. The low, fat heel of her shoes made a familiar thump sound when she walked. She started down the hall toward Andrea, her eyes slowly lifting from the floor to the doorway.

Ruth stopped in surprise, and it was as if she could see Andrea through the portal. "What are you doing in my house?"

"I—" Andrea tried to answer.

"Go on, get!" Ruth charged at her, fearless.

She lifted her champagne hand as if she'd crash the delicate glass into the intruder's head.

"Grandmama, wait." Andrea held up her hands. "It's me."

Ruth stopped at the doorway, eyeing the barrier. The music continued to play. She stared at Andrea's face. "Andrea?"

Andrea started to reach across the threshold, her hand trembling.

"Ruth, what is it?" Florence appeared from the kitchen.

Ruth glanced back, and the image instantly went away. The music stopped. Her grandmother was gone.

Andrea stared at the mansion's hallway. Ruth had seen her. She had looked directly at her and recognized her. What did that mean? Why would she be given a chance to step back into time? Should she have gone?

Andrea poked her hand through the doorway to the hall. Nothing changed. The portal was gone.

"Are ya all right?"

Andrea blinked at the man's voice. Kenneth walked toward her, his presence strange as it replaced the past.

"I thought I heard ya call out," he continued.

Andrea took a step back and glanced at the

protective barrier. Kenneth stopped by the doorway, following her gaze down. He did not pass.

Andrea took another step back.

"Ya have no need of this kind of protection in here," he tried to assure her. "No one in this house means ya harm."

"Who said I was afraid of what was in here?" she answered, noting he did not step past the line of brick dust.

"Are ya running from something?" he asked. "What did ya mean earlier when ya said ya had your own demons to deal with?"

"What do you really want from me?" Andrea refused to answer his question. Just like before, each time he spoke, she felt like they were dancing along a line and neither one of them was willing to jump across first. She didn't trust him. She didn't *know* him enough to trust him. And he clearly didn't trust her.

Kenneth had made it clear he didn't want her here. It was only his daughter's trap that had resigned both of them to this situation.

"Nothing. I want nothing from ya." He ran his hands through his hair in frustration. Why did she have the impression he was lying?

The man was attractive. There was no doubting that. At first, she'd been too shaken with fear to appreciate it fully. Now with him trapped on the other side of the door, she felt a stirring of interest in her stomach.

When they'd been in the office together with Jewel, she'd caught the scent of his cologne. The memory of it surfaced. There was something familiar about the smell, about him. She felt drawn to move closer.

"I think we can both safely assume there is something the other is not willing to say," Andrea said.

"So ya admit that ya are hiding something." Kenneth leaned against the hallway wall.

"I'll tell you mine if you tell me yours." It might have been a lie. Even as she said it, Andrea wasn't sure. She found it hard to concentrate. The donut she'd managed to stuff into her mouth earlier no longer was enough to stave off the growing hunger headache. But, to find food, she'd probably need to leave the bedroom.

"If I tell ya mine, I can't promise what the consequences will be for ya."

"Same," she answered.

"And if ya try to hurt my family, there will be a price to pay," he warned.

"Same," she said.

"I guess I lied. There is something I want from ya." He didn't move as he studied her.

"What's that?"

"The truth." Still he remained where he was. "And what do ya want from me?"

"Tell me why it is you can't step past the brick dust. It's clear your intentions aren't good."

"Who said I couldn't step across your enchanted brick dust?" He pushed away from the wall.

Andrea glanced down to the floor and back up at him in challenge.

He gave a small laugh and easily stepped inside.

Surprised, Andrea opened her mouth but no sound came out. She hadn't been expecting that.

Kenneth chuckled. "It's rude to enter a lady's chamber without permission."

She became acutely aware of standing in a bedroom alone with the man. The location seemed intimate.

"Did ya find everything ya needed?" he asked. If she wasn't mistaken, his words had become softer, lower.

"Yes. Thank you. Your sister's closet looked very expensive. I didn't want to borrow any of those clothes, so I found this." She gestured at the shirt and sweatpants.

Kenneth gave another small laugh. "Yeah, I guarantee if those were in Malina's drawers, they're just as expensive."

Andrea's eyes widened and she looked down at herself. "I can take them off."

When she glanced back up, Kenneth had a strange expression.

Realizing how the words could have been misconstrued, she corrected, "I mean, change out of them into something else."

Too late. The double entendre was there and would not be ignored as ideas sprang into her thoughts. The nearby bed was in her peripheral. Only a few steps away. One sweep of his hand would close the door to give them privacy.

Andrea shook herself from her runaway thoughts.

"What is it?" He lifted his hand, concerned.

Andrea realized she was frowning at him and it took a few seconds to get her thoughts back on track. "Um, I…" She took a deep breath. "I believe there are forces in nature that we cannot see or hear, but they guide us. I think I was guided here to try to help your family, but I'm not sure how much I can help with Jewel. You say she's not a demon, so I'm guessing possession, maybe? There are a few things we can try, but I'm not going to oversell my abilities."

Andrea thought of her first solo encounter, Mama Cecile. She hadn't even finished the first sentence of the banishment she'd planned. That little swamp shack was still there, waiting to draw in visitors to its misery. In many ways, Andrea had never left the swamp. Part of her soul was still there, hovering above dark waters inside a rickety shack. And now Mama Cecile had attached herself to her, haunting her.

Tick, tick, scrrich, tick. The mere thought of the sounds gave her nightmares.

But she was here now. Trapped. She had to try to help the MacGregor family, right?

Whatever magick was at play might not let her go until she did.

If she stayed, would Mama Cecile show up?

"I'll need to call a practitioner I know to make sure I have the right measurements and ingredients. They need to be precise for this ceremony. And—"

"My daughter is not possessed," Kenneth interrupted.

"I'm sorry. I know this is difficult to hear, but I think you know her abilities are not human," Andrea said. Was this man under a cloud of denial? "You do see that she makes things happen, don't you?"

"Of course I do." Kenneth's tone became hard. She noticed that happened whenever he acted like he needed to defend his daughter. He was very protective of the child. "Jewel is special.

She's not…" He ran his hands through his hair and paced toward the fireplace.

"I know you don't trust me, but I think you have to."

His eyes met hers, and she saw all the stress and worry he must have been carrying inside for a long time. He looked down, tapping the line of brick dust with his toe before glancing up to where the chimney would release its smoke.

"This house is protected," he said. "Ya don't have to worry about sprinkling brick dust and hanging charms. Nothing will happen to ya here."

"You keep saying that, but this is a big house. Even if you have the knowledge to protect it, there is a lot of ground to cover, which means a lot of tiny holes for things to slip past." Andrea noticed he'd changed the subject away from his daughter. Again.

"Twenty thousand square feet," Kenneth stated.

"I'm sorry?" She tilted her head, not following his train of thought.

"This house has twenty thousand square feet, give or take. Sixty-plus rooms. Then there are eighty-some acres of woods, a stream, a barn, walking paths, six acres of back gardens directly behind the house. I assure ya, we are aware of the size, and all but some of the back acres have adequately been covered. My brother Euann's one responsibility to this family is to see to the security."

"I'm not talking about security cameras and electric fences," Andrea dismissed.

"Neither am I, though he does like to play with his little techno-toys." Kenneth turned his back to the fireplace and leaned against the mantel. "I'm talking about magick. Real magick. Old magick. And if any of those were to fail, which is rare, then the extended family living here would be able to defend against a breach. We'd even protect the town if necessary. It's a little more difficult with the population not knowing they're being protected. My family started selling wind chimes and window charms made of ancient symbols. The locals think they're novelties, but they're hanging them around town for us."

"I see." Andrea nodded, believing to understand. "It's rare to find families who practice these days."

"There are probably more than ya think. Ya just need to know how to look."

"Don't you mean *where* to look?"

"No, I mean how." His eyes focused on her. "But if it makes ya feel better to dirty the floors with brick dust, feel free. No one will stop ya. A little extra never hurt."

Considering she was almost out, if what he said was true then that was one less thing she needed to worry about.

But then, what was with the portal to the past that opened up in the hallway, *inside* the so-called protected house?

There were so many unanswered questions.

"So what exactly does your family believe? Animism? Folk magick from Scotland?" Andrea didn't know much about the beliefs in that part of the world.

"Animism, sure that's part of it," he said.

"So—"

"We're warlocks," he stated.

"Oh, so—"

He lifted his hand, cutting off her words as a sphere of blue formed in his palm. "Warlocks."

"Warlocks," she repeated, leaning over to see the bottom of his hand. Surely this was some kind of fake magic trick from a novelty store. A trigger hidden in a ring, perhaps?

He balled his hand into a fist and extinguished the light. Then, lifting his hand so she could study it, he turned it around to show it had been no trick. With his fingers pointed upward, he wiggled them, causing streaks of blue to surround each digit. Then, pointing at his other palm, he trans-ferred the light to his other hand. He formed a light ball and tossed it back and forth between his palms before saying, "Catch."

Andrea stumbled back but automatically lifted her hands as the ball flew toward her chest. The light landed in her palms, tingling her skin and moving as if alive. The sensation was amazing, as it shot an electric current through her entire body, giving her a boost of energy. But that wasn't all it did. It heated her in pleasurable—*albeit ill-timed*— ways. She lifted the light closer to look inside the depths but it dissipated into a thin trail of smoke that slithered across her face like a lover's caress.

Her palms were hot and red from where she held it, and she shook her hands to cool them.

"That's…" She couldn't find suitable words to express how she felt. "Wow."

"Your turn," he said.

"I can't do tricks like that." She felt a little lightheaded. "My family isn't that kind of magick. Our powers come from all around us. We know how to mix the right ingredients, arrange the right talismans, and call upon the past for help. Folk magick."

"There are several forms of folk magick. Which is yours?"

"My family is from Louisiana, Creole coun- try." Andrea sat down on the edge of the bed, looking at her hands. They still tingled. Her heart was beating a little faster than usual, thumping in her ears.

"Voodoo?"

"That's a religion, similar in some ways I guess, but not the same thing," Andrea answered. Everyone always assumed that first. She thanked Hollywood movies for that. "We're closer to hoodoo, like you said, folk magick."

"Ya don't sound like ya are from Louisiana," he observed.

"I'm not. I was raised in Illinois. My grandparents had moved there when my mom was born. My parents died in a house fire when I was seven. My mom saved my sisters and me before going back in for my dad. After that, Grandmama Ruth took me in. She'd returned to New Orleans to be close to her family after my grandpapa had died. Grandmama and her first cousin, who we called Aunt Florence, raised us."

"We? Ya and your sisters?"

"Two younger sisters—Angela and Annie. They still live there. The female gene is strong in my family. Not many boys. Even though males technically carry the deciding chromosome, but... never mind. It is what it is." Realizing she was doing most of the revealing, she said, "What about you? Your mom was telling me about some of the people, but there seems to be a large extended family living in this mansion with you that she neglected to mention. Do all your cousins, aunts, and uncles live here as well?"

"The idiot with the car keys does. His twin brother Cory lives in town with their younger sister Maura. They just moved here and are looking at taking over the motel."

"The Hotel motel?" Andrea asked.

"Yeah, that's the one."

"Fletch at the front desk will be excited about that," Andrea joked.

"Don't think I've met him." Kenneth went toward the window she'd been at earlier and looked down over the yard. "Others come and go on business, but Aunt Cait and Uncle Murdoch spend most of their time here. Raibeart—"

"Right, naked guy," Andrea said.

"We've tried to enchant his clothes to stay on him, but it never works," Kenneth admitted. "And if he does end up proposing, just say no. Trust me."

"Noted."

"Uncle Fergus and Aunt Donna will be coming back from Europe soon with their English bulldog, Traitor. That dog is like a child to Fergus. Margareta and Angus, my parents who you've met. Me, Jewel, my brother Euann, his wife Cora—"

"I'll stop you there. I'm not going to remember all of those names without having met them," Andrea admitted. "I don't know if I could live with my entire family like that. I can barely stay a week in the same house with my sisters before a screaming match starts."

"Ya know that saying, takes a village. I think someone in the MacGregor line took that a little too seriously. We've been moving around like this since the 1300s. We're nothing if not codependent."

"I think it's nice that you all are close. That's how families should be." Andrea stood up from the bed. "Though, saying that, I again admit that my sisters and I cannot live in the same house for too long. At best, we could maybe live on the same city block. If that block was busy and we didn't run into each other every day. I love them deeply, but they're trying. Then again, our houses were never the size of an actual city block. Growing up, we weren't even given our own bedrooms."

"Trust me. Space does not make sibling rivalry go away. We have a ledger book of old grievances waiting to be avenged. Which reminds me, I'm due to replace all of Raibeart's scotch with tea and saltwater."

Andrea grimaced. "That sounds awful."

"He laced all the marshmallows in my cereal

with a swearing potion," Kenneth said. "Try holding a board meeting compelled to say the word *fuck* every other sentence. Luckily most of the cursing was in Gaelic so they couldn't understand what I was saying."

Andrea laughed. She leaned against the bed to keep from swaying on her feet, trying to ignore her hunger. "I've never heard of a swearing potion, but my first question is, why is a grown man eating cereal with marshmallows in it?"

"It's delicious," he defended. "And it's endorsed by tiny sailor elves."

"Wouldn't putting swearing potion in his scotch be more tit-for-tat?"

"No." Kenneth waved his hand in dismissal. "He swears in meetings all the time."

Her stomach chose that moment to growl. The loud noise was unmistakable in the quiet bedroom.

Kenneth reached into his back pocket and pulled out his cellphone to check the time. "It's late. Have ya not been offered something to eat?"

Andrea shook her head in denial.

"I apologize. I assumed my ma had seen to it."

Andrea averted her gaze.

"Tell me she gave ya lunch." He frowned, as if silently answering his own question. His eyes narrowed in on her. "Please don't take offense to this, but ya look a wee bit sickly, as if you're about to fall over. When is the last time ya ate something?"

Andrea rubbed the bridge of her nose. Her fingers were still warm from the light ball. "I had intended on eating donuts all day, but your ma interrupted my plan."

"And ya tease me about marshmallows in my cereal."

"They were free from the motel." She crossed her arms over her chest. "I live on a budget." That was a gross understatement. "And I don't say no to free food."

He kept staring at her. She didn't like the expression on his face. It appeared to be a cross between confusion and pity.

"Come with me." Kenneth motioned for her to go toward the hallway.

Andrea paused before forcing herself across the barrier into the upstairs hall. He strode before her, outpacing her hesitance.

"With our schedules of late, we all fend for ourselves when it comes to breakfast and lunch, and sometimes dinner. You're welcome to anything ya find, and if ya have a preference, just give me a list and I'll make sure the groceries ya want are delivered."

When she neared a cracked bedroom door,

she heard Raibeart's voice joined by Jewel's laughter. His words, which she guessed to be Gaelic, were impossible for her to understand.

Andrea ran past the open door, not wanting the child to see her. She held her breath as she rushed, glancing back to make sure Jewel did not come after her.

As she turned to watch where she was going, she crashed into Kenneth's chest. He stumbled as he caught her against him. He held her, even when it was no longer necessary for him to do so.

"Ya are terrified of her." The words sounded sad.

Hell, yes, she was terrified of the powerful, kidnapping, warlock child.

Andrea didn't answer.

"A nanny frightened of her charge." Kenneth's words were soft, as if he had not intended her to hear them, even though he had her head pressed against his chest. The beat of his heart thumped against her cheek.

A nanny sexually attracted to her boss, she thought in dismay. That scenario rarely ended well, even when magick wasn't involved.

She drew her arms between them, pressing her forearms into his chest to break his hold. He seemed reluctant to release her.

"The kitchen?" she prompted. Maybe the

lightheadedness was low blood sugar and not raging hormones.

A woman could hope.

"Of course." He nodded. This time he walked beside her, keeping an eye on her as they made their way downstairs.

Andrea tried to force him to walk faster by quickening her pace. She could think of little else knowing that food was close.

Chapter Seven

Shadows moved across the ceiling. Their shapes kept Andrea awake. Her attention focused on how they changed, as if answers to unasked questions would reveal themselves if she were patient enough. Sometimes life required a person to stop and pay attention. She felt the pressure of the pillow against the back of her neck, the smooth sheets against her naked legs, the weight of the heavy comforter against her chest.

She'd been so hungry that she'd ate three sandwiches. The food helped to clear her thinking. The way she saw it, she had three problems: Mama Cecile, mysterious portals, and the whims of a toddler. She wasn't sure which was the most frightening.

Well, there was a fourth problem, but being

attracted to your boss was more of a human issue than a supernatural one. After dinner, Kenneth had given her a tour of the house and her mind couldn't help but find all the secret locations in which they could have found a private moment.

Her vision blurred and her eyelids drifted closed.

Tick.

Andrea gasped, forcing her eyes to open, unsure if she'd heard the noise or if it was the beginning of a dream.

The ceiling shadows appeared to form a misshapen arrow pointing toward a window. Andrea pulled the comforter off her body. She wore the t-shirt as a nightgown. It barely covered her underwear. There were more clothes in her car, but when she'd tried to leave the house, the front door would not open.

She leaned against the wall, hiding her outfit behind the curtain as she peered at the lawn. The moon wasn't full but there was enough light to see shadows. Two short figures ran across the grass toward the parked cars, one chasing the other. Before reaching the drive, they changed directions, running around the house out of her eyeline. It looked like kids playing.

Andrea frowned, whispering, "Where do you two think you're goin—?"

Tick.

The noise came from behind.

Andrea spun around to look at the dark room. She hadn't imagined it. Her back pressed into the curtain. She held her breath, listening for signs that she was not alone. When nothing happened, she leaned forward.

Movement caught her attention, forcing her to turn. Red-rimmed eyes stared at her from directly outside the second-story window. The moonlight silhouetted strands of hair.

Mama Cecile.

Andrea inhaled sharply. Her throat squeezed, keeping her from screaming. The apparition's finger lifted to the window pane and tapped...

Tick. Tick.

...then scratched down the wooden frame.

Scrrich.

The sounds did not match the actions, but that hardly mattered.

Tick, tick, tick...

The spirit's hand stopped but the sound continued. Mama Cecile stared at her, the intensity unmistakable.

Tick, tick...

The window began to shake. Andrea looked down to see the line of brick dust vibrating. The powder danced forward and began to sprinkle onto the floor as it fell from the windowsill.

Tick, tick, tick….

The sound began to pick up pace, each dreaded dull note causing that ball of fear to twist inside her chest.

Andrea wasn't sure how she managed to convince her stiff legs to move, but she inched backward toward the door. The vibration became louder and faster.

Tick-tick-tick-tick…

"I meant no disrespect," Andrea whispered. "I mean no harm. I wish… I wish…"

"No!"

Andrea yelped as Jewel called out behind her.

"Bad!"

The shout was followed by the sound of small running feet padded by carpet. Jewel darted past her toward the window.

"Bad old lady. Bad!"

Andrea reached toward the child to stop her but found it difficult to move. The girl's words were clearer than the babbling she'd done before.

Jewel reached up and slapped the window with her hand, even as she was too short to see out.

Mama Cecile's eyes lit with fire and then her face disappeared in a swirl of smoke.

"Not nice!" Jewel slapped the window a few times. The girl turned around and smiled. Her eyes were filled with flames.

The tightness in Andrea's chest began to lighten and she inhaled a deep breath. She wasn't sure how much more her heart could take.

"Holy crap," Andrea whispered. "I was just saved by a two-year-old."

"Tsk, tsk." Jewel clicked her tongue as if trying to mimic the ticking sound. Her hands lifted into little claws. "Tsk, tsk, tsk."

Andrea lifted her hands before her in defense and backed away from the magickal kid.

Jewel giggled. "Tsk. Scroot. Tsk."

Chapter Eight

It didn't matter how many times Kenneth discovered his daughter missing from her bed in the middle of the night, a small parental panic still filled him. He hated to admit his ma was right. He needed help with Jewel. When the others weren't around, he was lucky to get in two hours of sleep in one stint.

Too bad the help he now had was terrified of him and his daughter. He'd tried to act like he didn't notice, but most of the time Andrea stared at him as if she waited for him to throw a fireball at her head. At least she took the knowledge of real magick without having some sort of episode. That was something. With her background, it would keep the rest of the family from threatening to erase her memories. Unless it was a tiny two-second incident, like a woodsman seeing one of them throw an energy ball, the erasing process never went smoothly. Humans needed memories to connect their emotions.

He stepped barefoot through the hall from his daughter's room, digging the bracelets out of Jewel's discarded leggings. For a while it worked to put the bracelets inside her clothes so she couldn't kick them off, but then she learned she could just take off her clothes and do whatever she wanted.

He had tried to get a message to the maker of the bracelets, Jewel's maternal grandmother, but Trina Castelaww had yet to answer his plea for help. He had left a message with one of Jewel's uncles, but they'd warned him that Trina was still in mourning and would not be available anytime soon.

Kenneth's ma would be livid if she found out. Trina and her sons had attacked the MacGregors. To be fair, Trina thought Kenneth had kidnapped her phoenix daughter. None of that mattered to his ma. Margareta would never admit it, but she saw Trina as a threat to her position as favorite grandmother.

"Come out, come out, wherever ya are," Kenneth said. The incantation didn't always work, especially when Jewel didn't want him to find her, but it was worth a try.

A tiny flash of blue light zipped past him toward Malina's bedroom.

"Dammit." Kenneth hurried to where Andrea slept, hoping his daughter didn't have her held hostage in playtime. The door was open and he knocked lightly on the frame.

The bedding was disheveled but no one slept on it. A sliver of light came from the cracked bathroom door.

"Bat." Jewel's voice came from the bathroom.

"Jewel?" Kenneth went toward the door. He knocked lightly. "Jewel, honey, it's not bath—"

The door inched open under his knock. His eyes met Andrea's. She sat in the tub with his daughter. Massage jets ran at full force, churning the water so the tub filled with bubbles. Andrea wore a dark t-shirt. His daughter wore a sparkly pink swimsuit with a glitter butterfly on the front.

"Da, bat," Jewel happily announced, her head surrounded by a growing white cloud of bubbles.

"I'm so sorry," Kenneth said.

"It's my fault," Andrea answered, holding the child's waist for support when Jewel would jump in the water. "It was the only thing I could think of to distract her from pretending to be a levitating monster."

"She's not a monster."

"I said *pretending*," Andrea insisted. "I know she's not a monster. She saved me from one."

Kenneth started to smile, but realized she wasn't making a joke. "What do ya mean?"

He didn't give her time to answer as he went to the bedroom to check. Each of the MacGregors had been born with unique talents, what they called their burden. Kenneth happened to be skilled at incantations. Like his brothers, his burden was that he was also a shifter. Somewhere in their ancestry, a relative had been struck with some kind of rogue magick that caused a mutation. His parents didn't like him calling it a mutation, but it was the only way he could explain the claws trying to grow from his fattening fingertips in response to his protective feelings.

Erik was a cat, Euann a fox, Niall a wolf, and Iain a bird—all sleek animals. Kenneth ballooned out to a whopping one-thousand pounds in the form of a Kodiak brown bear. It's not something he enjoyed and it had been years since the animal scratched the surface. The last thing he wanted was Jewel seeing her da in his animal form. It would give the girl all kinds of ideas. However, now, he found his eyes shifting to see better in the dark and his chest broadening in warning.

Traces of magick lingered in the air, but that was hardly uncommon in a home filled with warlocks. And, with this being Malina's bedroom, it was even more so. Every outfit hanging in his sister's closet had been materialized from magazine pictures. Fading magick clung to the walls like hairspray residue.

Kenneth could detect no one in the room with him so he went to the window overlooking the front lawn. A concentration of small round marks marred the window pane. He rubbed his hand over the glass and found they'd been made on the outside. The brick dust also appeared as if it had been blown into the room from outside.

"Reveal yourself," he said.

A couple of tiny blue light came from within the trees, which he could reasonably assume were deer. No other living creatures were around.

"Rawr!" Jewel pretend roared.

He turned in time to see his bubble-covered daughter running at him. He instantly caught her and lifted her into his arms. She proceeded to smoosh kisses on his cheek while transferring bubbles onto his face and shirt.

"I don't see anything," Kenneth said loud enough so Andrea could hear him in the bathroom. His daughter had been known to conjure things in her past lives.

Andrea appeared in the doorway with a towel

wrapped around her waist. Her t-shirt clung to her body. Kenneth averted his gaze.

"I thought I'd have more time before she found me," Andrea said.

Kenneth frowned and drew his eyes back to hers. "Who?"

"A few years ago, I came across an angry spirit in the swamp. Locals had nicknamed her Mama Cecile. She's been chasing me ever since." Andrea crossed to the window and drew the back of her hand through the brick dust to straighten the line. "She was coming for me tonight but Jewel told her to go away."

"What does she want?" That didn't sound like the typical haunting. Spirits didn't normally chase people across the country unless they'd stolen some kind of sacred object. He glanced at her ear to where the white hair had been growing. She'd colored it dark brown to hide it.

"To finish what she started. I was the one who got away." Andrea studied him holding Jewel.

"Is that what happened to your hair?" he asked.

She self-consciously touched the locks.

"My Aunt Cait can help. Trust me, ya won't be the first one in this family to prematurely gray. She can reverse what was done, if ya want." He didn't mean to make her uncomfortable. "I only mention it since ya don't seem fond of the white. I think either way would be pretty on ya."

If he wasn't mistaken her cheeks flushed a little at the compliment. "You need to convince your daughter to let me go. It's not safe for all of you if I stay here."

Kenneth took a deep breath and thought for a moment. Then, shaking his head, he stated, "No."

He moved to carry Jewel toward her room.

"What?" Andrea hurried after him. "What do you mean no?"

"No. This is clearly why ya were brought here. It's not safe for ya to leave." He kept walking. To his daughter, he said, "Jewel put on your fuzzies."

Jewel's magick flared and the swimsuit disappeared to be replaced by zebra-print fuzzy pajamas.

"That's a good girl. Now we're going to play the sleeping game. See if ya can beat me to dreamland, little love." He placed Jewel on her bed. She was asleep before he slipped the bracelets over her legs and tucked her in.

Andrea waited for him at the door. He lifted his finger for her to stay quiet as he left the room. He pulled the door shut.

Jewel might have been dry, but Kenneth's shirt was still wet from holding her. Without thinking, he pulled it over his head and wadded it in his hands.

Andrea gasped, staring at his chest as he stood before her in cotton pajama pants and nothing else. They were in the hallway but the house was quiet and they were alone.

"What happened to you?" she whispered, not hiding the fact she stared at his scars. They formed a series of broken spirals in his flesh.

"Mountain magick," he answered. "It's a long story."

"I have time." Her hand fisted around the towel at her waist, holding it up.

Instead of answering her, he studied her face. "That is where I know ya."

Andrea frowned. "Uh…?"

"When Jewel was a baby, ya came into our home." It had taken him awhile to remember where he'd seen her before. His brain had been half frozen at the time as he'd been thawing out of his ma's magick.

Andrea slowly nodded.

"Ya saw me."

It wasn't a question but she nodded again.

"Why are ya back now?" he asked. "Why did ya come then?"

"For me it was yesterday," she said. "I heard a baby crying in my motel bathroom and when I went to investigate, I was brought here… apparently two years in the past. I wanted to help you, but I didn't know how. I don't know why any of this is happening."

"I dreamed of ya," he admitted. "I couldn't remember your face, not clearly, but there was something about your…"

"My…?" she prompted when he took a deep breath and didn't finish.

"Your essence."

Her lips pressed together for a moment before she smirked. "My essence?"

Kenneth nodded. Even to him it sounded like a lame come-on line. Trying to start a romantic relationship with the new nanny-hostage wasn't the best of ideas, but the more he was around her, the more he felt the same awareness he'd had in his dreams.

This woman was special.

He knew her, felt her.

Her smile fell and he realized he'd been staring at her.

"I'm sorry I didn't free you," she said. "I wanted to."

"Ya couldn't have," he dismissed. "The only cure for that spell is time."

Andrea picked at her wet shirt, peeling it away from her skin only to have it adhere once more.

"Follow me. I have a dry t-shirt ya can borrow." Only after Kenneth went to his bedroom next to Jewel's and opened the door to invite Andrea inside did he realize what he'd done. He must be out of practice with women. "Is this inappropriate?"

Andrea arched a brow and passed by him. "Offering me a dry shirt? I don't think so."

Kenneth automatically lifted his hand toward the fireplace, lighting it with a spark of magick. He'd intended it for warmth, but the orange glow cast his room in an intimate light. All that was missing from his unintentional seduction was sexy music and wine.

"Do you mind if I...?" Andrea gestured to the bottle of scotch on a tray near his bed. "It's been a long day."

Correction: sexy music and scotch.

"Help yourself."

Andrea went to pour herself a glass. "This isn't one of those salty tea bottles, is it?"

Kenneth chuckled. "No, it's safe. I stole it from Raibeart's stash. I was going to drink it and then refill it. He always has the good stuff."

She tossed back a drink and then coughed. As her body jerked the towel slipped off her hips. Lace panties hugged her ass. Kenneth couldn't look away.

"Whoops." She reached to pick up the towel. "Well, that's slightly embarrassing."

Blood rushed down his body to settle in his groin. She wrapped the towel around her waist, but the image of her thighs burned into his brain.

It had been so long.

He took a deep breath, trying to steady his shaking hands.

So fucking long.

Though the memory of them were hazy, he was pretty sure his dreams had led him down this path several times. She'd been just an idea, a face he couldn't see clearly, but the attraction was real.

"Kenneth?" She tilted her head as she stared at him, holding the glass out and swinging it side to side so the liquid undulated. "Would you like one?"

He couldn't look away. A surge of emotion filled him, more powerful than anything he'd felt in a very long time. It caused him to step toward her.

Kenneth wanted to speak, to find his reasoning, but instead his hand lifted to hover by her cheek. He was not this man. He didn't have sex with women he'd just met. Not anymore.

He was responsible now.

He had responsibilities.

He…

He…

Kenneth watched as she reached back and set the glass on the nightstand without looking. She leaned into him. He was unable to think or move. Her hand lifted, mimicking the hovering gesture of his.

"I'm not sure what I'm doing," she whispered.

Andrea looked at his mouth, hesitating as he hesitated.

They stood for a moment, transfixed.

"I—" he started.

Her mouth lifted to his, cutting off his words. His fingers glided into her hair.

As her hands moved to his chest, he felt the towel slide against his pajama pants to land between them on the floor. Her fingers danced along his scars. She trembled in his arms, falling into him as if her knees weakened.

Their kiss deepened, tongues moving closer as their bodies pressed together. Warlocks were lustful by nature, and he'd been denying that part of himself for a long time. Her sexual energy fed his starved magick, giving him a rush of power. That's not the only thing it fed. His arousal lifted to press heavily against the cotton pants.

Kenneth kissed her like a man in need of his *fíorghrá.*

Fíorghrá? Why was he suddenly thinking about true love? He wasn't prone to boyish fantasies.

Probably because he'd been without sex for so long and had been dreaming about sleeping with this woman for two years.

A tiny voice whispered in the back of his mind, telling him he should take a step back and make sure this is what she wanted. Even as he intended—well, at least he liked to think he'd intended—to do just that, she turned him so that his back was toward the bed and pushed.

Kenneth landed on the mattress. The bed was high from the ground, so his legs dangled over the side. Andrea crawled over him even as he moved more fully onto the bed. When he lay flat, he stopped his progress, as did she. Her legs parted over his. The heat from her body teased his shaft and he pulled her to him.

Kenneth gasped at the shockwave of pleasure that flooded him at the intimate contact. She kissed him again, her desire unmistakable. Expensive scotch flavored her lips. The wet shirt felt both cold and warm as it clung to her torso.

He lifted her shirt, yanking it over her head and tossing it aside. Soft breasts beckoned his fingers, and he couldn't resist a small squeeze before sliding his hands up her neck to cup her face.

"Look at me," he commanded, needing to see the dark depths of her eyes. He searched her for signs of enchantment or magick. Kenneth's body had been denied for so long. He wanted to believe this was real, but he needed to be sure.

"What is it?" she asked, her hips making tiny movements against him. Her eyes were bright and reactive.

"Just checking." He caressed a breast as he pushed at his waistband with his other hand.

"Condom," she said.

Kenneth let a tiny surge of magick take over his hips. His pajamas disappeared. "Already done."

She glanced down for confirmation and laughed. "Handy trick."

"I'm full of them."

Andrea stripped from her panties, maneuvering them from her sexy legs. The contact of her thighs against his nearly made him lose himself. The firelight caressed her chest, a visually pleasing display as she took his shaft and drew it to the opening of her sex.

"Why do I feel like we've been here before?" She held herself over him, not joining their bodies completely.

"We've been here in my dreams," he answered, knowing without a doubt that he'd felt her before now. Her skin was familiar, the curve of her hip. It was as if he'd memorized it many times.

"Yes. Dreams." She nodded. Her hands pressed against his chest. "We've done this before. I always felt so safe with you. Like now."

She slowly accepted him into her body. The tight glide of her sex made him want to use his magick to take over the pace. Her soft moans kept him transfixed in place as he resisted the urge, giving her complete control.

Kenneth cupped her breasts. His fingers glided over hard nipples before he let his hands roam to her waist. The agonizingly measured way she eased onto him was enough to drive a man insane. He couldn't take it. The need was too much. His hands trembled as he pulled and thrust his hips at the same time, drawing her fully to him.

"Oh," she gasped, the sound so very feminine that it nearly caused him to prematurely climax.

A cry of pleasure escaped his lips. She began to rock, rotating her hips in tiny circles as he held her against him.

Oh, fuck, he wanted this.

Soon the small thrusts weren't enough. He lifted and dropped her hips so she rode him. With each fall her breasts bounced. The sight caused him to force her down harder so that he could watch them move.

Sweat beaded her flesh and his hands slid. She took over the pace, setting her own hard rhythm. Each thrust was confident and she was not afraid of what she wanted from him. The driving pleasure began to fill the ache that had been growing inside him. Andrea was perfection. She was everything. In this moment, she was all his. The beauty of their joining was too much to resist and he was unable to stop the sudden explosion of his release.

Andrea gave a small cry, trembling and shaking over him as if his climax gave her permission to find her own.

Her fingers worked against him, the nails lightly scratching his flesh. She breathed hard. Her expression was caught between pleasure and pain.

Kenneth had not meant for this to happen. There had to be so many reasons why their having sex was a bad idea. But, for the life of him, he could not think of one.

How could perfection be wrong?

How could this moment be wrong?

Andrea fell onto the bed next to him, stretching her arms over her head with a contented moan before lying on her side. Her finger traced one of his scars.

"This was probably a mistake," she said, as if reading his thoughts.

Kenneth took a deep breath, trying to still his racing heart. "I was thinking the same thing."

Her finger stopped. She arched a brow as she gave him a pointed look. "I don't regret it."

"I was thinking the same thing," he repeated, completely entranced by her.

Andrea chuckled. "I'm happy to hear that."

He reached to hold her cheek in his palm and begged the gods that this did not fade into a dream. It seemed impossible that a man could be so lucky as to have her looking at him the way she gazed at him now, so open and without regret.

"The way I see it," she wagged her brows playfully, "the mistake has already been made. There is no going back. I think we should do it again. Only slower this time."

At that, he grinned and rolled onto his side to face her. "Ya know, love, ya must be a mind reader because I was thinking that exact same thing."

Chapter Nine

Andrea felt safer than she had in a long time. The darkness outside was kept at bay by the orange glow of the fireplace. Crackles from the burning wood were enough to drown out any noise that might have tried to invade from the night. Kenneth lay on his back with the kind of smile that said he was pleased with himself. Considering the fact that her entire body was numb with relaxation, he had a right to be pleased.

"I can't get over it. Why does being with you feel so familiar?" Her head rested on his arm. She felt him flex beneath her at the question.

"I thought we decided our dreams have connected us." He gave a small smile.

Andrea laughed. "Do you believe that you are the man of my dreams?"

"Aye." He nodded.

Andrea lifted onto her side. "As strange as it sounds, I think you may be. When I showed up at your house yesterday and you were stuck as a statue, there was something familiar about your..."

"Essence?"

"Yes, your essence." As funny as the word was, there was no other way to describe it. She'd known him on some level for the last two years, years she'd spent on the run from Mama Cecile. That couldn't be a coincidence. "Yesterday I went into your past, we connected somehow and your past self bonded with me, and that anchored a thread that has linked us for the last two years. That sounds a little crazy when I say it out loud."

"No crazier than everything else around here." The arm she'd been resting on shifted and Kenneth caressed her shoulder, gliding his fingers everywhere he could reach.

They fell into a comfortable silence. Andrea studied her surroundings. The dark wood mantel and doors contrasted the lighter wall. Everything in the room seemed centered around the giant bed.

With the size of the flames in the fireplace, the room should have been unbearably hot, but the temperature stayed pleasant—not too hot, just a touch chilly. A portrait of Kenneth in a kilt hung over the fireplace. It had been one of the first things she saw when she'd entered the room. His hair had been longer and he carried a set of bagpipes. The background looked to be the inside of a castle. From the small peek she was afforded of his chest under the portrait's white shirt, she detected the scars were missing.

"Tell me about these." Andrea touched his scarred chest. "Did you have them done on purpose?"

"No. Body modification was never my thing," he said.

"Who is responsible for giving them to you?" She leaned over to kiss his chest before continuing to trace. There was no mistaking the marks were deliberate. By the scar tissue, some of the cuts had been particularly deep.

"Geneva, Jewel's ma, was the daughter of a mountain witch from West Virginia. I met her in a bar over a glass of enchanted moonshine—only I didn't know about the enchanted part. The next thing I know I'm naked and she's performing a ritual over my body. After the bloodletting, we…"

"Had sex," Andrea prompted, thinking his modesty strange yet endearing. He hadn't been a shy man in bed.

"Yes, sex." Kenneth drew in a long breath

before letting it out slowly. "Hours later, Geneva's dead and I'm running through the forest with a newborn, trees are in flames, and the mountain witches are coming after me with enchanted pitchforks."

"The witches killed her?"

"She killed herself, but not before she forced me to promise I'd protect our daughter from magickal threats. When the others came to take the baby, she threw herself into the fire she'd started. Nearly thirty years later, here we are."

"That's so—wait. Thirty years?" Andrea leaned away from him. A baby born hours after conception? Thirty-year-old toddler? That sounded like some kind of fairy tale, not real life.

Then again, she'd been two years into his past yesterday.

It was enough to give her a migraine if she tried to reason too hard.

"Geneva was a phoenix. She passed that power to Jewel. It was the only way she could end her life. I can't blame her for wanting to do it. No person should have to carry that much pure magick inside of them. I think the responsibility must have caused her to go mad."

Andrea didn't speak. His expression saddened as he talked about it.

He placed his hand over hers on his chest.

"These scars help me to be Jewel's protector. It safeguards me from most of her magickal influence. My daughter is very powerful and immortal, but that immortality comes with a price. I have watched her die three times now only to be reborn. I will do whatever I can to make sure she does not start wishing for the same end as her mother."

"That's horrible. I'm sorry." Andrea rolled onto her back and stared at the white-painted beams forming squares on the ceiling. "That poor girl. I couldn't imagine what it would be like to reset my timeline and have to go through childhood again."

"She doesn't remember her past lives. Perhaps that is a blessing," Kenneth said. "It's difficult to get a phoenix to adulthood. I haven't even gotten her to last into her teens. Once there, she should be able to steady her powers, but one accident and I'm raising a baby again. I miss all my daughters. I want them back, just as I want Jewel as I have her now."

Andrea shivered. She tugged the blankets out from underneath her and pulled them over her body. "I can see why you're protective of her— not only because she's your daughter, but as her parent, you mold what kind of person she will become. She's fortunate to have you, but moreover, the world is fortunate you have *her*. I can't imagine the devastation she'd do with the wrong mentors directing her moral compass. I can also see why your mother said you were housebound."

Kenneth chuckled, though if she had to guess she would say the sound was more annoyed then amused. "Actually, my daughter is not keeping me here. I'm grounded. My ma discovered me trying to leave with Jewel to go into hiding. She and my aunt cast a spell trapping me inside. They claim it's for my own good."

"What happens if you try to leave?"

"Nothing fun." He stood from the bed, pulled down the covers, and then crawled in next to her. "Now it's your turn. Tell me about your family."

"I—"

"Andrea Marie Breaux, you come out here at once."

Andrea gasped at the sound of her grandmama's voice and sat up. She pulled the covers to her chest in a panic. The tone was quiet but firm, as if Ruth didn't want to yell.

"What is it?" Kenneth sat next to her.

"Didn't you hear that?" Andrea asked.

Kenneth tilted his head. An inner light flashed in his eyes as he listened. He slowly shook his head. "I don't hear anything."

"Don't you go haunting your grandmama," Ruth's

voice continued. *"You're not too old for me to summon you back for a spanking."*

"Can I borrow that shirt now?" Andrea reached out her hand as she stared at the door. Her grandmother wasn't a prude, far from it, but Andrea couldn't help but feel like a child about to get into trouble.

A shirt materialized in his hand and he handed it to her. She scurried off the bed. Andrea tugged the shirt over her head, grateful that it was long enough to cover her thighs. As she pulled her hair from inside the neckline, she hurried toward the door.

She heard Kenneth moving behind her. Her hand trembled as she reached for the knob.

Tick, tick.

Andrea gasped and jerked her hand back. She stepped away, not opening it.

Kenneth brushed past her and was pulling open the door before she could find the voice to stop him.

Ruth stood there, in the same dress as before but no longer holding her glass of champagne. Andrea had to lean around Kenneth to see her.

"I don't hear anything," Kenneth said, not appearing to notice her grandmother.

"Look at you," Ruth said. "Come closer."

Even though this doorway faced a different

direction than Malina's room, the portal was the same as before, stretching into a hall from the past.

"Wait here." Kenneth walked through Ruth and turned to go down the MacGregor hallway. He disappeared into her grandmother's wall.

Andrea stared at Ruth.

"You look like you've seen a ghost," Ruth said.

"Did you find her?" Aunt Florence appeared next to Ruth and smiled as she looked at Andrea. "Oo, you turn out pretty. To tell you the truth, we weren't so sure. Our Andrea is long-legged and gawky like a stork." She lifted one leg off the ground and drew her hands to her sides like wings to mimic the bird for a few seconds before laughing and waving her hand in dismissal. The party had been going on for a while and both ladies had been drinking.

"Don't tell her that," Ruth scolded.

"What?" Florence gestured so that her hand encompassed Andrea. "She's grown out of it."

"But our Andrea is sleeping in the other room, and you don't want her hearing you talk like that," Ruth insisted.

"What's happening?" Andrea didn't dare pass the barrier. "How are you here? How are we talking?"

"Thank goodness you showed up tonight. Our

Andrea is too young to hear about the kind of power you're up against. We're here to warn you," Ruth said. "*Cher*, you're in trouble."

"What makes you think I'm in trouble?" She crossed her arms over her chest, feeling a chill run up her spine. There was no way they could know about the future in which she now lived.

"The spirits spoke and we listened," Florence said.

How many times had Andrea heard that in her youth? It had been her aunt's excuse for nearly everything she wanted them to do. It was her version of "because I said so."

"*Clean your room. The spirits spoke and we must listen.*"

"*Go to the store for me. I'm out of milk. The spirits spoke and we must listen.*"

"*Take this paintbrush and give the fence a fresh coat. The spirits spoke and we must listen.*"

"And what did they say?" Andrea asked.

"Darkness is coming for you." Florence shared a look with Ruth. "What? It's true."

"You don't have to be so blunt about it," Ruth scolded. "*Cher*, listen to your grandmama now. I don't know what it is, but you caught the eye of a powerful force. If it hasn't already, it will attach itself to you soon. And when it comes, it will come fierce."

"What kind of force?" Andrea thought of Mama Cecile and Jewel. Both were powerful. Both were attached to her. "Do you mean a spirit?"

"All we know is that it is strong magick and it will alter you forever. You better watch yourself," Florence warned. "This kind of magick will gobble you up and ask for seconds."

"Here." Ruth reached behind her neck and unfastened her necklace. The medallion was made out of an old coin and supposedly blessed by a powerful priestess a few generations back. "Take this."

Ruth didn't give Andrea a choice as she tried to reach across the barrier to hand it to her. Ruth's hand disappeared, not making the journey across. She pulled back, frowning as she still held the necklace.

Andrea reached to take the necklace but her hand disappeared and she jerked it back. She could not cross the time barrier. Apparently, she was not meant to travel into this past.

"It's probably best you can't give it to me," Andrea said. "You'll need it."

"Don't tell me. I don't want to know the future," Ruth said.

"Forget that," Florence interrupted. "Tell me all about the future. Am I still alive?"

Andrea gave a small, hesitant nod to affirm that she was. "You both are, but you need to quit smoking sooner. We know about your smokin' spot behind the shed."

"That's for rituals," Ruth blatantly lied. As a kid, Andrea would have believed it.

"Is John going to propose or what?" Florence asked.

"John?" Andrea frowned, not remembering a John. She didn't know her aunt had a boyfriend.

"She's talking about her stories," Ruth dismissed.

Soap operas? Andrea shook her head with a laugh. "I have no idea what John will do."

"That's the problem, isn't it? No one does," Florence huffed. "He doesn't have the good sense—"

"We don't know how much time we have," Ruth stated, cutting her off. "Andrea, don't say any more about our futures."

"Grandmama, why are the spirits warning you in my past? Why not now?" Andrea asked.

"Andrea?" Kenneth asked. His voice sounded close but she couldn't see him. "Who are ya talking to?"

"Give me a minute," Andrea dismissed him.

"A minute for what?" Florence asked.

"Grandmama, why now?" Andrea insisted.

"I'm guessing whatever it is that has found you is not going to want us helping you," Florence answered. "Spirits don't see time the same way we do, so they're warning us now."

Kenneth walked through her aunt and came into the room. "Andrea, no one is there."

"Shh," she shushed him. "It's my grandmother and aunt."

"Who are you talking to?" Ruth asked.

"It's my," Andrea glanced at Kenneth, trying to find the right word before she muttered, "boyfriend."

"Boyfriend?" Kenneth repeated, sounding surprised. She took his arm and pulled him away from the door so she could better see.

Ruth and Florence instantly looked over her outfit, as if seeing it for the first time. Florence laughed, clapping her hands. Ruth shook her head and clicked her tongue.

"I don't see a ring on that finger," Ruth scolded.

"Oh, hush." Florence swatted Ruth's arm. "Since when do you have to be married to have a boyfriend or two?"

"What's happening?" Kenneth whispered.

"They're commenting on my lack of wedding ring." Andrea crossed her arms over her chest. To her relatives, she said, "If you're done teasing me, I need your help. I think I know what the powerful threat is you're talking about."

"Where are you?" Ruth asked.

"In Green Vallis, Wisconsin," Andrea answered.

"Jewel is not a threat," Kenneth stated.

"Write that down," Ruth ordered to Florence.

"With what? Do you think I keep a pen up my —" Florence was cut off as Ruth swatted her. "I was going to say skirt."

"Andrea, my daughter is not a threat to ya." Kenneth moved as if he'd stop the conversation he couldn't see or hear.

"No one is talking about Jewel," Andrea dismissed. She wished they'd all stop trying to talk to her at once. "You sent me to the swamp, and I tried to stop Mama Cecile. I failed." Andrea frowned and looked at the floor in shame. "I thought I could handle it. The signs started and I was close."

"No." Ruth shook her head.

Suddenly, all of their words came at her in a rush.

"That doesn't make sense," Florence said.

"We'd never send you to do that," Ruth insisted.

"What are they saying?" Kenneth asked.

"What were you thinking, *cher*?" Ruth demanded.

"Spirits like that don't have this much magick," Florence said. "This warning felt much more powerful."

"Is it night time there?" Ruth asked. Andrea managed a quick nod. "Then give us a call in the morning. No need to interrupt our beauty sleep. We'll write down—"

"This isn't right," Florence put forth.

"What are—" Kenneth started to repeat.

"Please stop. I can't hear all of you when you talk at once." Andrea closed her eyes and held up her hands. When she again looked, the doorway was empty. The portal to the past was gone and she was alone with Kenneth.

"Dammit. They're gone." Andrea went toward the door and lifted her hand to reach through the barrier slowly. Nothing changed.

"So what was that? Are ya a psychic?" he asked.

"I don't know what kind of magick that was but I'm pretty sure I'm not doing it. Like I said before, portals started appearing in doorways at the motel. They took me here when I saw you as a statue. Then tonight, they started showing me into the past, to my grandmother's house from when I was a kid. The spirits warned them that danger is following me. I need to call them tomorrow. I think they'll have information about Mama Cecile. She's clearly more powerful now than she was back then."

"Ya have come to the right house. My family will protect ya." Kenneth pulled her to his chest and held her. "I won't let anything happen to ya, Andrea. I promise."

"You don't owe me anything." Andrea leaned back so she could study his face. She wanted to accept his help, but she couldn't bring her troubles to his family. It didn't seem right. He had to think about his child.

"But I thought ya were my girlfriend." He grinned.

"I had to tell them something." Andrea gave a small laugh as she gestured at her outfit.

"No take-backs." He brushed his hand over her cheek.

"So you want to be boyfriend and girlfriend after one day?"

"It's been a strange day," he said with a glance at the door. "Technically, we've known each other two years, more or less." He brushed her hair back from her face. "Andrea, I won't lie. I've told ya my life is complicated, but I'm also not squeamish when it comes to what I want. I like being with ya. I feel comfortable with ya. I feel like I know ya from another life, maybe the dream world. Standing here, with ya, feels right. That is all I need to know."

"Just like that?" Andrea knew, logically, that relationship decisions shouldn't be made so quickly, and yet she knew what he meant. This felt right, as if every day she'd lived had been leading to this moment.

"Aye. Just like that."

"I'm not good with labels," Andrea admitted.

"Boyfriend, girlfriend, lovers, friends…" Kenneth shrugged. "I don't care what ya call this thing we've started. A word won't change how I feel or how I act, unless ya tell me ya don't want my attentions. Living with magick is complicated enough. I have no need for games when it comes to relationships."

Andrea smiled at the simple honesty of his statement. "I want your attentions."

"Then it's settled. You'll stay here and let us help ya fight this Mama Cecile." He urged her to walk with him toward the bed. "And what happens between us will be what is meant to happen."

Andrea nodded.

"Ya have to be exhausted. There is nothing more we can do tonight. Come to bed. Tomorrow we will find a solution." His concerned gaze swept over her face.

It felt as if a weight lifted off her at his words. She'd been on the run, alone, for two years, knowing that fate was closing in on her. Now, to have help, to have someone who understood she wasn't crazy, was more than she could have hoped.

At the idea of sleep, she yawned and nodded. "All right. We'll try it your way but only because I don't have a better idea."

Chapter Ten

Andrea woke up alone in Kenneth's bed. There was safety in the weight of the covers on her legs, in the quiet of the room. In the haze between wake and sleep, she wasn't sure which was the dream world. The smell of him lingered on the pillow. Light streamed in through the window and the flames in the fireplace had died.

There was something to be said about the aftermath of sex. With the tension eased from her body, she'd been able to fall into a deep sleep, which helped her stress levels come down immensely. She could say without a doubt this was the best she'd felt since before that night in the swamp.

As reality trickled over the dream, she became more fully aware of her surroundings. Kenneth had left folded clothes on the dresser for her. The jeans and stylish gray sweater weren't hers, but they fit perfectly. After her shower the night before, her hair had dried into a mass of curls. She combed her fingers through the locks, fluffing them so they looked even.

When she opened the door, she wasn't sure what would greet her on the other side.

"Hey, Ken, do ya have the stain remover?"

A man approached looking down at his naked stomach. His skin was dyed a dark shade of blue and his hair green. He wore a kilt and nothing else, revealing that the coloring most likely covered all of his body.

"I opened a new soap and our wench of a sister left me a present." The man glanced up and stumbled in surprise. "Ken? Did Malina get to ya too?"

"I'm not Ken," Andrea said.

"What?" The man appeared surprised. "Ya mean…" He grinned, trying to look behind her toward the bed. "He here?"

Andrea shook her head.

"*Was* he here?"

"Hi. I'm Andrea." She stopped his inquiry before it became any more awkward.

"Oh, sorry, I'm Erik. Kenneth's brother." Erik

grinned. Something caught his attention, and he glanced down the hall. "Rory, come here."

"I've heard of blue balls, but that's taking it to another level. What did ya do to piss Lydia off?" Rory asked.

"Kenneth has a woman," Erik said.

"It's not official. I still have a chance." Rory appeared next to Erik, his teasing smile fading. "Or not."

"Morning, Rory," Andrea said.

"Hey, Andrea. Tell me I'm not too late." Rory gave a dramatic sigh.

"Sorry, it's not going to happen," Erik said for her, pushing Rory back the way he came. "We told ya, you're just not lovable."

"What do ya know, Captain Blue Balls?" Rory waved his hand in Erik's face as he came back to the door. "Ya only found someone because Lydia clearly did something bad in a past life that she needs to atone for in this one by marrying ya."

"Jealousy is never pretty, cousin." Erik slapped Rory's shoulder, before calling out, "Iain, come here. Meet Kenneth's woman."

"Ya are not supposed to refer to women like that," Iain's voice answered.

"It does make ya sound like a caveman," Rory agreed.

"Andrea, my apologies," Erik said. "Fellas, this is Andrea, she's Kenneth's *lady*."

"Much better," Iain drawled, giving her a quick wink.

Rory tried to push Iain and Erik behind him as he came forward. "Ignore them. They're Neanderthals."

"Wait," Iain said, as if just now noticing his brother. "Why are ya blue?"

"Malina," Erik said.

"Shampoo?" Iain asked with a laugh. "That'll do it."

"That's why I put all of my shampoos in ya guys' rooms. I'm not using anything she left for me." Rory gave a short laugh.

"This was yours?" Erik asked. "You're the reason I'm the color of a cartoon character?"

Rory chuckled and slowly began to back away from him. "What were ya doing showering here, anyway? Don't ya have a home to go to?"

"Not that my bathing habits are any of your concern, but I was helping Murdoch clear part of the acreage for a putting green. I thought I'd shower before returning home to my wife," Erik said. "Not that ya would know, but women like a man who bathes."

"Whoo, look at me!" Raibeart ran past in fairy

wings that matched the plaid pattern of his kilt. Jewel toddled along behind him.

Andrea was the only one who appeared interested in the scene. Iain merely stepped out of his uncle's way and said, "Good morning, little love," as Jewel ran past him.

"I'm going to see if Lydia has anything that will take this blue off," Erik said. "If I manage to resemble a human shade later, we should all go get drinks at Crimson—"

"Um," Iain shook his head, "Kenneth isn't getting out these days."

"Family dinner then." Erik strode after Raibeart. "Even better. Let Ma know she's cooking."

"Come on, Andrea." Rory hooked her arm with his and pulled her from Kenneth's room. "I'll show ya to breakfast."

"She looks smart enough to find where we keep the food." Iain fell into step next to them as they made their way to the stairs. Erik continued straight before disappearing into another room.

"Look at me, rightly flying," Raibeart yelled.

Andrea gave a small yelp as he jumped over the railing toward the marble floor. Her heart leapt in her chest as fear choked her. She automatically went to stop him even though she was too late. Jewel tried to follow him over. The child jumped next to the rail.

"No!" Andrea swooped Jewel into her arms and stopped the child from toppling over.

Raibeart gave a gruff laugh as he floated in the air, paddling his hands and kicking his feet as if swimming a few feet beneath the ceiling. Jewel wiggled in Andrea's arms. Blue sparkles erupted around them as Jewel disappeared.

Andrea made a weak noise. Jewel appeared next to Raibeart, mimicking the man's movements as the pair dog paddled in the air across the front hall.

"Um, we can explain," Iain said behind her.

"Magick," Andrea answered. "I know."

"Ya know?" Rory repeated, joining her by the railing. If she wasn't mistaken, the man actually leaned closer to her and sniffed. "What kind of magick are ya?"

"Did you just smell me?" Andrea leaned away from him.

"Nice perfume," Rory said.

"Um, thanks." She wasn't wearing any. "And I'm not magick. Not like this."

"Then like what?" Iain insisted.

"Folk." Andrea kept an eye on the flying duo while making her way to the stairs. She pointed at them. "Are you sure this is safe?"

"Probably not," Rory answered with a shrug. "But she hasn't hurt him yet."

"I meant for the child," Andrea corrected.

"Oh, sure. She's the one doing it." Rory took the steps two at a time. "Let's hurry before she decides we all want to fly to Neverland with the lost man-child up there."

Andrea followed Rory and Iain toward the dining room, careful to keep an eye on what was happening above them.

"Kenneth made pancakes." Angus sat at the table with a stack of twelve pancakes covered with blueberries. He cut into the top layers with a fork.

Rory went toward the kitchen. "Hey, Angus said there were pancakes. Where are they?"

Kenneth appeared in the doorway in exasperation. "Those weren't for ya, da."

"They were just sitting there." Angus hurried to take another bite.

"On a tray," Kenneth said. "I was making them for Andrea."

"Breakfast in bed?" Iain asked, his tone teasing. "Nice play, brother. Might I also suggest the carpet picnic."

"Signature MacGregor move," Angus agreed, before taking another big bite. "Women can't resist the indoor picnic."

Kenneth's eyes met hers. She smiled, but

before she could say anything, Rory reappeared with a fork. He stabbed a pancake from the top of Angus' stack and shoved it in his mouth.

"Back, ya animal." Angus poked Rory in the thigh with his fork.

Rory made a strange noise and laughed at the same time, even as he coughed to keep from choking on the food in his mouth.

Iain stole a pancake with his fingers while Angus was distracted. He rolled it and began eating away from his da's stabby fork.

"Thank you for making me breakfast," Andrea said to Kenneth as his family ate it.

"I should have known better than to leave it unprotected." He motioned for her to follow him to the kitchen.

A tray was on the counter with a glass of orange juice and a coffee. A napkin looked as if it had been folded at one point but had been knocked over. She pointed at the coffee. "Is this for me?"

He nodded. "Give me a minute. I'll remake the pancakes for ya. I hope ya like blueberries." Kenneth arched a brow. "And pancakes. I guess I just assumed, but if ya want something—"

"I love all those things. Thank you." Andrea supposed she could have politely assured him he didn't have to make her anything but she wasn't about to turn down food. Plus, the aroma floating around the kitchen smelled amazing.

He poured several ingredients into a bowl, not bothering to measure anything. Then, as he whisked, he said, "I'm curious about something."

"Yes, I would love it if your aunt can fix my hair color," she answered. "Mama Cecile turned it white."

"If that's what ya want. Either way, it'll be beautiful, but I wasn't going to ask that."

"I'm thirty," she said.

"I wasn't going to ask that, either," Kenneth said, "but if that is your slick way of asking me how old I am, I was born in 1589. Ya will have to do the math. I stopped keeping track."

Andrea started to laugh but realized he wasn't kidding. "That's only slightly intimidating."

That was a giant understatement.

"Were ya hoping for someone older?" He stopped whisking and winked before walking over to a griddle.

"Honestly?" Andrea bit her lip and nodded. "Yeah."

Kenneth laughed. "What I was going to ask was—"

"How is it a person like me comes to have roots in Louisiana folk magick?"

He lifted a spatula and pointed it at her. "That's the one."

"It's kind of a long story." She moved closer to him and leaned against the counter as she sipped her coffee.

"My favorite kind." He poured the batter onto the griddle and kept his attention focused downward.

"According to family legend my great-great-grandfather was for all intents and purposes a masochistic asshole who made his fortune in the cotton trade. No one has a kind word to say about the man, not even the few mentions I've seen in historical documents. He had several illegitimate children and even more mistresses. I don't know how it came to be or why, but he married a kind-hearted lady from Pennsylvania who was never happy living in the Deep South, and even less happy with her family's choice of husband for her."

"I've seen my share of arranged marriages. I prefer the ones made out of love," he said.

Andrea set the coffee mug on the counter. "After their first and only child was born, the wife, my great-great-grandmother, found out about his mistresses' children. It's said she treated all of the illegitimate siblings very well, including the ones he had with the servants. Asshole-grandfather didn't like it, and it's said his cruelty killed kind-grandmother's fragile heart. After she died, several curses were placed on him and he wasn't soon behind her. One of my great-grandmother's half-sisters came from a family of hoodoo practition-ers. Over the years, the family practice has shifted and changed, but that is where its roots come from."

"So the half-sister's family adopted your great-grandmother?" he asked, flipping a pancake.

"Not exactly. As heir to the fortune, my great-grandmother had plenty, but to repay the kindness of her mother, the family did look out for her and taught her folk magick to protect herself. To this day, the two family branches remain close." Andrea smiled. "Aunt Florence, one of the women I was talking to last night, is Grandmama Ruth's first cousin, the daughter of the half-sister. They grew up playing together and now live together."

He stacked four pancakes on a plate and handed it to her. "The blueberries and cream are by the tray."

After she scooped toppings onto her breakfast, Rory appeared in the doorway. Seeing her holding the plate, he instantly snatched it from her. "Thanks, Andrea."

"What?" Andrea blinked in surprise. Rory

disappeared before she could stop him. She turned to Kenneth. "But…"

"Welcome to my world." Kenneth chuckled. He had already poured four more onto the griddle.

"I thought my family was a handful." Andrea gave a small laugh and resumed her spot next to him by the counter as he cooked.

"Need a tall stack and a short stack," Raibeart announced from the doorway, holding Jewel.

"Tall 'tack," Jewel said.

"Make that two tall stacks," Raibeart said.

"Hot 'tuff," Jewel said, kicking her legs in excitement.

"Sorry, muffin, you're too young for the hot stuff," Raibeart said, carrying the child back to the dining room. His plaid fairy wings looked a little tattered as if he'd crash landed. "Whiskey coffee for me. Cocoa for the fairy princess."

"I'm not a short-order cook," Kenneth called after him.

"Not with that attitude, you're not," Raibeart answered.

"Yeah," Jewel piped in. "Not wit' that tattitdue!"

"Is it me or has her language skills advanced since yesterday?" Andrea remembered the child's gibberish when they first met.

"I hadn't noticed, but then I'm used to her little mental growth spurts," Kenneth said.

"Not that I'm complaining because I need a paycheck, but I don't think you need a nanny. Raibeart seems like he has the job well in hand." Andrea could tell Raibeart had a good heart, even with his naked drunken runs through the town and passing out in the public library. The man undoubtedly loved his niece, and she adored him.

"That he does," Kenneth agreed, "when he is around. Raibeart is a free spirit."

"Why do I feel like there is a story there?" Andrea asked.

"Not much of a story. Sometimes a mood strikes him and he goes a little mad."

"That might explain why I saw him being chased by an invisible badger when I arrived in town," Andrea said.

"Could be," Kenneth agreed.

"Do you have a water kettle? I can start the cocoa." Andrea waited as he pointed toward a cabinet. "You said he goes mad?"

"Aye. Sometimes, rarely, there are people born who act as a type of siren for a warlock's magick. It has to be the right warlock and the right human. We call them *inthralls*. They siphon off the warlock's magick and can use it for themselves."

The sound of happy voices came from the dining room followed by a burst of laughter.

"What does that have to do with Raibeart?" she asked.

"His lover was an *inthrall*. She drained him of his magick and his physical energy. It left him broken and a little crazy. The magick and energy recovered. His sanity was another story. He's been a bachelor ever since, who also happens to propose to every female he meets. He says he's convinced when he finds the right one, she'll say yes." Kenneth flipped a pancake. "That's not to say all *inthralls* are bad. Erik's married to his. It's worked out well for them."

"There could be something majorly wrong with a woman who says yes to marrying a stranger," Andrea warned. "Raibeart should be choosier in his future wife."

"For all we know, a hundred of them have said yes, but he doesn't remember." Kenneth handed her another plate with pancakes before pouring more.

She topped them, then went to the dining room doorway and called, "Order up."

"Mine!" Yet another MacGregor shot up from the chair to take the plate.

"How about ya give it to the child, Murdoch,"

Iain said, swiping it before Murdoch could lay claim to the food.

Kenneth arched a brow when she came back to the kitchen.

She gave a small shrug. "If you can't beat them, join them. I figured I'd just go with it. And it looks like we're going to need a lot more batter."

Chapter Eleven

"What visit?" Grandmama Ruth's voice was soft as it came through the phone. "Andrea, you're not making any sense."

Andrea walked away from her car parked in the driveway. It felt nice to be outside in nature, stretching her legs and breathing the fresh air. Rory had left her cellphone in the front seat but thankfully it was charged. She'd called her grandmother for information, but hearing her voice made Andrea realize how much she missed the woman.

A wave of emotion filled her and she couldn't answer right away. The overcast sky diffused the daylight so that everything was bright and it hurt her eyes to look up, but at least there were no signs of storms. She studied the looming mansion. It would seem that her decision to stay allowed her to leave the house, but she had a feeling if she ran, another portal would open up and drag her right back.

Kenneth had told her the mansion and surrounding grounds were protected, and as long as she stayed close, she should be fine. Andrea looked up at the window to Malina's bedroom. Protected or not, the spirit had been there. But, with the clear skies, none of the usual signs were present and she wanted privacy for this phone call.

She felt someone watching her and glanced to where the curtains moved. Margareta didn't bother to hide her stare.

"Andrea, are you there?"

"I'm here, Grandmama Ruth," Andrea answered. She walked past a large tree growing in the front yard toward the side of the house where Margareta couldn't see her.

"Where are you, *cher*? Are you safe?"

"Green Vallis, Wisconsin." Andrea could hear the worry in her grandmother's voice. "I'm staying with friends. Yes, it's a safe place. The MacGregors are like us."

"There used to be a MacGregor family with magick living down here years ago," Ruth said. "Same one?"

"Maybe. This family is from Scotland." Andrea turned the corner to go down the side yard.

"You said you were calling about a visit? What visit?" Ruth asked.

"I'm talking about when I was younger. You were with Aunt Florence and we spoke through a doorway in time."

"Is that happening?" Ruth asked, surprised. "Flo, get in here. Andrea says it's happening."

"What's happening? The wedding?" Florence's voice sounded far away. "We already know about that."

Andrea passed over the side yard between the forest and the house, unsure why she was compelled to walk in that direction. She saw movement in the trees and stopped, studying between the trunks.

"No, the other thing," Ruth said.

"The baby?" Florence asked.

"The other thing," Ruth insisted.

"The dance of the full moon?"

"The other thing."

"The chickens?"

"No."

"The banshee?"

"No."

"Burnt pudding?"

"No, that other thing."

"Well tell me. Don't make me guess," Florence grouched.

"The spirit with the time slip from when Andrea was a girl," Ruth said, as if Florence should have automatically known the answer. "We wrote it down somewhere in one of the old note-books. Check storage."

"Pipe burst ruined all that old stuff," Florence reminded her, sounding closer. "Besides didn't we already do that? Here, give that to me. Let me talk to her."

Swooshes and bumps came over the phone as the two ladies fought over it.

Andrea couldn't see anything coming from behind the trees and slowly moved toward the back gardens. She slipped between two trimmed bushes and made her way to the landscaped path.

"Andrea, it's Florence," her aunt said. "What you're going to want to do is look the spirit in the face, but not the eyes, and say the chant. Call upon your family magick and banish that bitch back to hell. Go ahead, I'll wait."

"Um, the spirit isn't here," Andrea said, "at least not right now. I don't know where it is."

"Oh. Well, next time it shows up, you do that," Florence said. "Do you have a pen?"

"Not on me." Andrea automatically glanced

around for something to write with, even as she knew there wasn't anything.

"Okay, then you'll have to memorize this list," Florence said.

"Go ahead."

"Cheese curds, string cheese, fresh mozzarella, and if you get the chance, there is a pizza place called Son—"

"Give me that," Ruth demanded, taking over the call.

"She's in Wisconsin," Florence protested. "We need cheese."

"Did you do the chant?" Ruth asked.

"When I first came across the spirit, I tried the one that said I meant no harm or disrespect but I don't think I was assertive enough because it didn't work," Andrea said. "You tried to hand me a necklace."

"What necklace?"

"Your silver coin one."

"Oh, that? I gave it to Annie years ago. She needed it for something," Ruth answered before asking, "Which spirit is it? Lady in white? Lady in black? Lady Kathleen? Mister in the lake? Monster of—"

"Mama Cecile," Andrea interrupted, reminding herself that for Ruth and Florence, the conversation had been decades ago.

"Why on earth would you try to send Mama Cecile to the afterlife?" Ruth shot back in surprise. "Cecile moved on before you were born. What's left at that place is death echoes—screeches and scratches to scare the tourists. Oh, *cher*, I think your imagination is playing up."

"But I've seen her. She touched me," Andrea denied, confused. "It's not my imagination. You called and told me that she'd been luring people to their deaths and that I needed to get to the cabin in the swamp to take care of it. You said I was the closest person and the signs said it had to be done that night. Aunt Florence told me the chant to say. You told me what to draw on the floor."

Tick. Tick.

The sound was soft, but she heard it in the trees. She stiffened, barely moving as she searched her surroundings. The skies had not changed. Nothing walked the path coming from the forest into the gardens. Leaves crashed in the trees as the wind moved through them, making it difficult to hear anything in the woods.

"Is that what you meant when you called to tell us you failed and then took off?" Ruth asked. "We thought you were having an essential crisis."

"Existential," Florence said.

"Existential crisis," Ruth corrected. "Why else

would you take off across the country to find yourself?"

"Who said I was finding myself?" Andrea frowned.

"Annie," Ruth answered.

Of course. Annie.

Andrea frowned. Her sister tended to fall on the more dramatic side. Also the one psychology class she took before dropping out of college tended to make her think she knew more about human nature than she did.

"I've been trying to keep Mama Cecile away from our family," Andrea said, still watching the trees for signs of anything abnormal. Insects hummed beneath the sound of the wind. "I went home and she followed me. You always said to trust my instincts, and they said to run, that if I stayed, you all would be in danger."

"We never told you to exorcise Mama Cecile," Ruth said.

"Because she's been crossed over for years," Florence inserted.

"And we would have heard if people were dying in the swamp because of a spirit. She's just a swamp legend told to tourists these days, a bunch of made-up ghost stories. If we had sent you on such a task, we would not have sent you alone, *cher*." Ruth chuckled. "You weren't our best student when it came to such things."

"No, she wasn't," Florence loudly agreed.

That made no sense. Andrea distinctly remembered the phone call. She remembered questioning their reasoning in asking her to do it. She remembered the urgency. She remembered writing down instructions. Hell, she even remembered she'd been two bites into a pizza delivery when the phone rang.

"You called me and told me to go," Andrea insisted.

"Whoever sent you, it wasn't us," Ruth continued, "and whatever marked you wasn't the spirit of Mama Cecile. What you're talking about seems to be a manifestation of something much more sinister."

"And personal," Florence piped in.

"If it's borrowing the shape of Mama Cecile and using the legend to scare you," Ruth continued, "then—"

"Tell her it's personal. The phantom chose her," Florence insisted.

"It's personal," Ruth said.

"I heard her," Andrea answered.

"Tell her—"

"She heard you, Flo, shush," Ruth admonished.

Tick.

Andrea turned around, unsure if she heard the warning sound or just imagined it. She was always on edge and it was sometimes hard to tell reality from fear.

"If what you say is true, how do I know this conversation is real?" Andrea asked.

"Cause Grandmama knows all your secrets, *cher*," Ruth said. "I know about when you stole ingredients from my cupboard trying to make a love potion for that bucktooth little Timmy down the street."

"Made him sicker than a dog," Florence inserted.

"It was for his older brother," Andrea protested.

"I know about the time you wanted nothing but peas for dinner because someone told you it would make your boobs grow bigger. I know you were mad that your mom got you a red bike when you wanted a blue one. I know—"

"Fine." Andrea stopped the stroll down memory lane. "You're you."

"Good to know. At my age, I'm not always so sure," Ruth joked.

The wind in the trees picked up and the temperature felt like it dropped a few degrees.

Tick, tick.

"Grandmama, it's found me. I hear it in the trees," Andrea whispered, cupping her hand over the phone. "What should I do?"

"Get inside and find a safe room," Ruth ordered. "It's easier to control smaller surroundings."

Andrea started to obey. A childish giggle came from the woods, followed by the sound of running feet over broken twigs and leaves.

"Crap." Andrea turned back to the forest. Her heart beat fast with fear. She wanted to run inside and hide. "I think kids are playing in the forest."

"Get them inside," Ruth ordered. "We don't know what we're dealing with. They could be in danger."

Andrea made a weak noise and nodded her head even though her grandmother couldn't see it on the other end. "Call you back." She hung up the phone and listened to her surroundings. She inched slowly toward the trees.

"They don't know," she heard someone whisper.

"You shouldn't be out here," Andrea said, torn between not yelling too loud but trying to be heard. "You need to come inside. It's not safe. Uh…" She glanced around trying to think of something that didn't sound insane. "The weather is going to get bad."

With her words, the wind seemed to pick up.

"They don't know…" the voice said again, the words trailing off.

"I do know you're there. I can hear you. Come inside." Andrea tried to sound stern, hoping it would jar the girl into listening.

"They don't know that we're here." The girl's voice came from another direction, singing softly this time.

"But their hearts will fill with fear," a second girl answered from the opposite direction, as if the two flanked her on either side.

"They did try to send us back," the first sang.

"But we slipped in through a crack," the second answered.

Andrea couldn't see from where the voices were coming. A chill worked its way over her. She backed slowly toward the house, hoping the door would be unlocked.

"You should go home," Andrea said, her voice not as firm as before. "I'm sure your parents are wondering where you are."

"They all thought that we were dead," the first said, her tone lower and filled with growing anger.

Andrea searched the gardens for movement.

A tug on her arm caused her to cry out in surprise. Andrea spun around. A young girl with dark blonde curls stood beside her, holding tight to her sleeve.

The girl wore a white dress with a petticoat under the skirt. A smile stretched across her innocent face, and she sang in a whisper as she finished her friend's half of the verse, "But we will kill them instead."

The child giggled, her face decaying as she became transparent. Andrea jerked away. The girl's form crumbled before disappearing.

Andrea stumbled back. These children didn't need her help. She turned to run into the house.

The girl had reappeared, blocking the path to the door. Her twin joined her, wearing the same innocent expression and white petticoat dress.

Tick. Tick.

The phantom was close and the ghost children blocked her quickest retreat inside.

"Help," Andrea mouthed, the sound not coming out.

"Andrea!" Kenneth's shout came from within the house. She saw him darting past a window.

Tick, scrrich, tick...

"Stay back!" The thought of him running into danger propelled her into action. She charged the ghost children as she sprinted for the door.

"Andrea," Kenneth called again.

Andrea cried out in fear, blocking her face

with her arms as she ran through the spirits. Freezing temperatures blasted her skin, and the air smelled like death. She wildly flung her arms to push the feeling away.

The spirits didn't stop her and she kept going. Yellow sparks erupted like fireworks in the doorway. The shock of their sudden blast caused her to stumble. She tried to focus past the light.

Kenneth was at the heart of the magick. He held the door open. His lips were parted as if to scream but no sound came out. His panicked expression didn't change. He was a statue like the first time she'd seen him through the portal.

A dark cloud appeared to her right, taking the form of Mama Cecile. Kenneth's frozen body was left exposed. Andrea ran as fast as she could before slamming into his chest to force him back.

An icy hand grabbed her wrist, but she slipped from the grasp as she made contact with Kenneth.

Their bodies pitched into the house. The door slammed shut behind them. Andrea braced herself for the jarring pain that was sure to come when Kenneth's hard body struck the floor. They hit with a loud thud, but instead of pain she fell through him and the world faded to black.

Chapter Twelve

Andrea's body disappeared from her consciousness. She couldn't see, couldn't feel a physical surrounding, couldn't hear or speak. All she had were her thoughts and the sensation of panicked emotions building where her chest should have been. If she had to guess what being a ghost felt like, this would have been relatively close.

Mama Cecile had killed her, or rather whatever was pretending to be Mama Cecile. When the phantom touched her arm it had felt different than the ghost children. The phantom was pure magick and intent. Andrea had felt the life pulling out of her.

She wasn't ready for death, but she was not surprised by it. It had been coming for her since that night in the swamp. That didn't change the sorrow now consuming what was left of her entire being.

With the knowledge came clarity. There was so much she wanted to do. She'd never traveled outside of the United States. She'd never wrote a book, a dream she'd secretly held since she was a teenager. She'd never been in love.

Kenneth.

Maybe she had found love.

The swirling of emotions began to focus themselves, pulling from her like a thread. Light appeared, a soft warm glow radiating from within. Her body returned, her senses numbed but there.

Strands of light snaked from her chest through the darkness, seeming to stretch into eternity

"Andrea," Kenneth said behind her.

When she turned to him the blackness of their surrounding lightened. They were in the MacGregor home, standing near the back door. She reached for him, intent on pulling him to safety. Her hand fell through his, unable to make contact. Thinking she missed him, she tried again, only to realize her fingers passed through him. She lifted her transparent hand, able to see a foot through her skin.

She frowned. The foot wasn't at the right angle, but it was her shoe. She drew her hand back for a better look. Her body laid on top of

Kenneth's from when she'd knocked him over. He was in the same position, arm reaching for a door-knob that was no longer there. Her limbs sprawled at odd angles over him.

Her eyes rounded and she willed the image to go away.

Crap.

She really was dead.

"It wasn't supposed to happen like this," she whispered, finding it difficult to speak.

"What happened?" Kenneth asked, drawing her attention away from their bodies.

"I was wrong about the entity. It's not the spirit of Mama Cecile. I called my grandmother and she said Cecile had been crossed over decades ago. She said they never sent me. What-ever it is lured me to the swamp and is using the legend of Cecile to scare me." She stared down at her body. "I'm not sure why. What if the portals were used to lure me here by Mama Cecile and not Jewel?"

"That actually makes more sense than a loca-tion haunting suddenly deciding to chase prey across country." Kenneth ignored their bodies on the floor. He was as transparent as she.

"You seem to be taking this pretty well." Andrea found herself drifting closer to him. She wished that he could hold her. She ached for physical contact, a touch of a hand, anything to tell her she could still feel the world.

"I've had a lifetime to become accustomed to paranormal threats," he answered.

"A long warlock's lifetime," she noted.

Kenneth nodded. "We'll get to the bottom of this."

She barely heard him as she pressed her hands together, seeing them touch but not feeling her skin. This wasn't right. She knelt by her body, trying to pull her arm.

"Andrea?" Kenneth asked. "Are ya listening."

"I don't want to be dead." She tried to insert her arm back into her body. It didn't work but she kept trying. Panic filled her. "No. No. No. No."

"Och, what are ya doing, lassie?" Raibeart appeared in a doorway wearing a kilt and leather bands on his forearms. A slash of tartan crossed his naked chest from left shoulder to right hip with a strap leather crossing the other direction to hold a sword against his back. Black paint slashed around his eyes and down his cheek. He appeared ready for medieval battle.

Andrea looked at him in surprise when he met her gaze. Was he coming to fight the phantom?

"Stop this nonsense. Get back in there." He lifted his hand and began tapping the top of her head. She felt his touch. "Get in there. Go on."

Raibeart forced her head down as he pushed her into her body. She felt her skin slipping around her like a latex body suit. Her lungs filled and she gave a high-pitched gasp for air as she scrambled to her feet. She felt her arms and face.

"I was dead," she said. "I was—"

"Not dead," Raibeart corrected. "Just a little undead. We've all been there."

"Kenneth!" She turned to where his spirit had been standing but couldn't see him.

"Come on, your turn." Raibeart gestured to Kenneth's statue on the ground. He made a series of motions that would have looked insane if she didn't know what he was doing. He kicked his foot sideways about the height of Kenneth's ass.

"What can I do?" Andrea asked. He ignored her.

"Get your arse back into…" Raibeart jammed the heel of his hand downward as he muttered to himself. "Your. Stubborn. Arse."

Raibeart took a deep breath as he stepped away from Kenneth. Andrea waited but Kenneth didn't move.

"What's wrong with him?" Andrea knelt beside him. His face was locked in concern, as if he still yelled for her. She touched his hair, trying to brush it back, but it didn't move.

"Eh, laddie, get up." Raibeart nudged

Kenneth's thigh with the toe of his boot a few times before chuckling. "He must have really made them mad this time."

"Who?" Andrea put her hand on Kenneth's chest but was unable to detect a heartbeat or breathing.

"I'm guessing this is the work of his ma and Aunt Cait." Raibeart seemed more amused than concerned. He leaned over his nephew and mocked Kenneth's shocked expression before laughing. "They weren't happy when he tried to take that sweet baby into hiding. It would have taken some powerful magick to trap him in the house like this. That kind of magick takes strong conviction and emotion to keep going. A woman intent on protecting a baby would just about do it."

"What about a father protecting his child?" Andrea frowned. "Doesn't that count? If he thinks it's best to leave then...?"

"Aye, sure, that counts, but women have a connection to life that men will never know. Ya carry it inside ya. That gives ya a special kind of power, one that does not take actual magick to work, a force ya can tap into with a fierceness. Witness a ma protecting her baby, or a grandma doing the same." Raibeart glanced around the room before snapping his fingers. A tube appeared in his hand. He went to his knees next to his nephew.

"Will that wake him up?" Andrea asked, trying to see what the man held.

"Nah. Nothing I can do about that. It wasn't my spell. My guess is he'll be like that for a few hours at least." Raibeart chuckled as he pulled the tube apart.

"What are you…?" Andrea frowned as Raibeart twisted a tube of orange-red lipstick and began swiping it along Kenneth's lips. "Hey, stop that!"

"There's a pretty lad," Raibeart laughed. "Ya think I don't know ya have been dipping into my special scotch."

Andrea snatched the lipstick away from him, getting it all over her fingers.

"Careful, love, that stains." Raibeart's grin widened. The color was smeared around Kenneth's lips like a little kid getting into his mother's makeup drawer. Raibeart stood and studied his nephew. "No need to be too protective. Kenneth knows he had this coming."

"And who are you protecting?" Andrea glanced meaningfully at his attire.

"This?" Raibeart reached behind him to touch the hilt of the sword. He grinned. "This is for wooing. I've got a date." He wagged his brows and his voice dipped into a seductive whisper, "I'm going to offer to show her my *sword*."

Andrea bit back a laugh of surprise.

"And when she says yes—"

"Oh, no, I don't need to know the rest," Andrea cut him off.

"Sorry, love. I didn't mean to make ya jealous." Raibeart gave her a look of remorse. "But I can't marry ya. My nephew's heart would break. I don't have many rules, but that's one."

Andrea pressed her lips tightly together to keep from laughing. The fact she could even think of smiling at a time like this was surprising. "I understand."

"No, don't ya cry. Ya must find a way to carry on, sweet one. Kenneth's a good boy," Raibeart assured her. "Doesn't know to ask for help, so make sure ya ask for the both of ya when the time comes. Now, why don't ya leave the bear rug where he's at and we'll get ya a stiff drink."

Raibeart turned to leave.

"Wait, I think I need help." Andrea glanced at the back door. "And I don't think it's safe to go outside."

Raibeart crossed to the window and looked at the back gardens. "What are the troublesome twins doing back here? Who let them out of hell?"

"You know the ghosts?" Andrea hesitated

before going to the window. "They said they wanted to kill the family."

"Oh, aye, those hellions run amuck causing problems. They're like a bad case of termites, eating and gnawing. Irritating at first but dangerous in the long term without an exterminator. We'll exorcise them. Again." He lifted his fingers and waved toward the back yard. He mimicked their singsong voices. "Ya can hide, ya can seek, we're going to send ya to hell to bake, ya little minions."

"I thought this home and grounds were protected," Andrea said. When she looked past Raibeart to the gardens she saw a faint shadow of Mama Cecile's shape. The two ghost girls held hands as they stared at the house.

"It is, from the usual," Raibeart agreed. "They're not usual. Those two will take a very special recipe."

"And the other one?" Andrea stared at the phantom.

"What other one?"

She pointed toward the shadow.

"Oh, love, ya don't have to make up threats to keep me from my date." Raibeart patted her arm. "If it's that painful for ya I won't go. But ya are going to have to accept..." He motioned to Kenneth's fallen statue.

"That's not—" Andrea tried to protest.

Raibeart put a finger against her mouth. "Shh."

Raibeart winked before backing away. He placed his hand over his heart and then began to sing a jaunty song in a language she couldn't understand. His voice softened as he walked from the room.

"No offense, Kenneth, but your family is weirder than mine." Andrea gazed over the garden. The shadow and ghosts had disappeared, but she wasn't about to leave him unprotected.

Chapter Thirteen

Being frozen into a statue wasn't as "fun" as it sounded. It was much, much worse. And incredibly boring. Plus, as he regained feeling in his skin there was an itch along his inner thigh he couldn't scratch.

Kenneth was unable to speak or move, but his mind slowly pulled from a dream state to an awareness of his surroundings. He watched Andrea as she stood by a window gazing at the back gardens. She tapped her fingers on the glass. He wanted to get her attention but all he could do was move his eyes. Though, if he had to be frozen with only one thing to look at, Andrea's ass wasn't a bad view.

"Please call me if you find out anything," Andrea was saying into the phone to her grandmother. "Yes, I promise I'm all right. I'm some-place safe. Please don't worry. They know all about magick here." She paused. "Yes, I promise I'll call. I love you both, too."

Her arm dropped and he assumed she hung up the call.

In his current helpless state, he had ample time to think. Andrea was here for a reason. He believed that. Whether it was fate, or his daughter's magick, he wasn't sure, but he wanted her here. When he was near her, he felt something beyond constant worry and fear. He felt whole.

That didn't mean the fear had left him. If anything, it grew. She had needed him to help her and he'd been trapped in the house. He could not protect her while in his gilded prison.

"I was told ya needed to speak to me," Margareta said from the doorway. From his position, he couldn't see her but he knew his ma's voice. "Why aren't ya with Jewel?"

"I offered. Cait said she needed her for a picture," Andrea answered. "Besides, I thought it best someone stay in here with Kenneth."

"I hadn't realized Cait was home. She's prob-ably having an artist paint Jewel's portrait." Margareta appeared near his feet to study him. She shook her head in disappointment like she silently chided a naughty child. "Cait is very particular about her family portraits."

"Your and Cait's spell almost cost us our lives," Andrea stated, her tone hard.

Margareta's expression tightened but she didn't turn to face the woman as she continued to stare down at him. She lifted her hand and gestured. A tissue floated to her fingers and she leaned over to swipe at his face. When she lifted the tissue so he could see, it was covered in smears of red-orange. It was evident one of his relatives had gotten to him. He could only imagine what his face looked like. To him, she whispered, "Not your shade, my son."

"You need to release him." Andrea's gaze bore into the back of Margareta's head. "I know you're afraid he'll leave, but that's what children do. They grow up, and move out, and raise their own families."

Margareta frowned. "I'm sure ya mean well, but we are not a normal family. There is protection in numbers. Jewel needs to be kept within the family fold. That arrangement is none of your concern."

"Isn't that her father's decision?" Andrea insisted. "How is trapping him inside these walls protecting Jewel? You have to know that's not right."

"I know that I will do anything to protect my family." Margareta turned and he could no longer see her face. Her hand balled into a fist around the tissue. "They may not like it, but I'll do what I think is best."

Kenneth struggled against his statue prison but was unable to break free. He tried to direct his thoughts toward his mother, begging her not to throw a fireball, even as he knew she would not be able to read his mind. Andrea had picked an argument with the wrong MacGregor.

"Does it look like your son is protected?" Andrea clearly didn't sense the danger she was currently facing.

"Ya are paid to entertain my granddaughter, not worry about my son." Margareta's hand balled into a tight fist.

Kenneth struggled harder, but it was no use.

"Someone needs to worry about him. Look at him." Andrea placed her hands on her hips. "He's literally defenseless. Your little power trip has made him a sitting duck for an attack. If Raibeart hadn't of come along and shoved our souls back into our undead bodies who knows what would have happened."

Well, hold on a minute. He wasn't *literally* defenseless. And he would have been able to reverse the out of body experience once the petri-fying spell weakened a little.

He hated not being able to defend himself.

Andrea nodded toward the window. "There is danger out there. Right there. In your backyard. It wants to get in. What happens if it does?"

"We protect—" Margareta's voice rose as she placed her hands on her hips to mimic Andrea's stance.

"This is not protection." Andrea's tone lifted to rival his mother's. "This is insanity."

"This is what is best. The very same hour Jewel came into her powers someone tried to get to her. Kenneth was indisposed and if I hadn't of held the child who knows what would have happened. I didn't see her face, but I chased the threat out of the house. We have stepped up the protection spells since that day. My granddaughter needs us whether my son wants to admit it or not," Margareta said. "I love my son but—"

"I love your son, too," Andrea argued back before gasping. She covered her mouth. Her eyes darted to his. "I mean…"

Margareta's posture relaxed. Kenneth wished he could turn his head to see Andrea better.

"I mean…" Andrea lifted her hands to her side and shrugged.

"Ya mean ya are in love with my son," Margareta said with a nod. "I'll forgive ya for your willfulness. I respect a woman who will fight for her man."

"He's not my… But I mean, we haven't talked about…" Andrea appeared flustered. "I mean I could, maybe, someday. We just met, but there are dreams, and—"

"So ya don't love—"

"We're in danger," Andrea cut his ma off. "There is a phantom following me, or something pretending to be a phantom. She's outside and I don't know what she wants. It's not a normal spirit."

Margareta went to the window and looked out. "I don't see anything. Maybe ya should calm down. Come, I'll get ya a cup of tea."

"It's not there now, but it is here, somewhere. I don't know what it wants, but I get the sense it's not to say hello and come by for a friendly cup of tea," Andrea insisted.

"It's probably just Jewel. For whatever reason, she wants ya here. Ya said ya were brought by portal, well, there ya go. Raibeart probably told her a scary story and she invented a phantom to chase ya here."

Margareta might have tried to sound reasonable, but Kenneth knew his ma well enough to know she was irritated. If Jewel hadn't trapped

Andrea at the house, it was possible his mother would have shown the woman the door.

"I'll have a talk with my granddaughter about this and get to the bottom of what's happening, but I would remind ya that you're the nanny. It is your job to take care of her, not to dictate how I run my home."

"I thought this was everyone's home—" The words barely left her lips. A bright light flashed and Andrea disappeared.

Margareta gasped and looked around. She placed her hand on her hips as she stared down at her son. "Well, that was a little rude."

He couldn't defend Andrea or go after her, but he knew she didn't disappear on purpose.

"I don't mean to…" His mother rubbed her eyes. "I know I'm…"

Kenneth waited, trying to listen while she muttered to herself.

"Family is the only thing that matters. Losing a child was the hardest thing I've ever had to endure," Margareta said. "And ya wanting to take that baby away from me…" Her eyes were moist when she looked down at him but she didn't let the tears spill over. "I can't go through the pain of losing ya again. If ya leave and don't come back… If I don't hear from…"

Margareta pressed her lips tightly together and

shook her head, as if pushing her feelings aside. Kenneth willed her to check on Andrea, but his ma didn't leave.

"Now, what is this about danger outside in the garden?" She went to the window where Andrea had been moments before and looked out. Kenneth stared at the ceiling, willing his eyelids to thaw enough so he could at least blink.

Chapter Fourteen

Out of every place she could have materialized after being flashed from Margareta's anger, into a giant bubble floating around the front hall of the MacGregor mansion was not even on the list of imagined possibilities.

Yet, here Andrea was.

In a freaking iridescent bubble.

Over the polished marble.

She was terrified of touching the sides or moving around too much. The sphere swirled, the sides the same color as the carnival glass Florence collected. What if it popped? That was a long drop to the hard floor below.

"Oh, hey, Andrea." Rory passed under her bubble and gave a small wave at her on his way out the door.

"Rory, wait—" she called out but he didn't stop.

Her elbow bumped the edge of her prison, but instead of popping it sent her slowly drifting. The soft pinks and purples swirled on the transparent surface.

"Andrea, has Rory passed through here?" Erik stood by the rail. His skin was no longer blue.

She automatically pointed toward the front door. "Yes, but—"

"Thanks." Erik ran down the stairs, his heavy footsteps loud. He went to the door and shouted, "Rory! Get back here. Give me that phone. If ya post that picture, I swear I'll—"

The door slammed shut behind him.

Andrea tapped her hand on the bubble, trying to get it to drift closer to the floor. Her stomach did little flips at the height.

"Andrea, did—" Euann appeared where Erik had been moments before.

"Rory and Erik ran outside, but before you chase after them get me out of this bubble!" Andrea tapped her hands against the sides. She was beginning to feel a little lightheaded and wondered if oxygen wasn't getting through the translucent walls.

Euann arched a brow. "I was going to ask if ya saw Iain—"

A large eagle buzzed past Euann's head.

"Found him!" Euann yelled.

Murdoch and Raibeart ran in after the bird. Murdoch carried a large net. Raibeart brought a blow dart. Their kilts swished dramatically against their knees as they took fighting poses.

"Call Jane," Murdoch ordered. "Tell her Iain's in flight."

"Come back here, chicken boy," Raibeart yelled at the bird.

"Fly Uncle Chin-ken!" Jewel ran after Raibeart.

"Why did ya tell her about that?" Murdoch slapped Raibeart's arm.

"It was story time," Raibeart defended.

Andrea hit the side of her bubble harder to get their attention. Each breath felt more difficult than the last.

"Move over, love." Raibeart lifted his blow dart and tried to aim around her. The eagle swooped over her, then under.

Murdoch leaned over the rail and swiped his net. It bumped her bubble and she began to spin.

The front door opened. The image of Erik running in holding a phone passed her vision. His clothes were tousled as if he'd fought his cousin.

"Got it," Erik announced.

"Shut the door!" Murdoch and Raibeart hollered in unison.

"Uncle Chicken on the loose," Raibeart added.

Erik slammed the door shut. Andrea saw him looking up from below.

"Iain?" Erik yelled. "What are ya doing? Get down. Did someone call Jane and tell her to retrieve her dumbass husband?"

"Did it," Euann answered. "She's on her way."

"I got this." Raibeart held the blow dart to his mouth and tilted his head to follow the eagle.

"Shit!" Jewel called.

"Did she say…?" Euann asked.

"*Shift*, little one," Raibeart corrected, not taking his lips from the weapon.

"Shif'!" Jewel giggled. She pointed her finger at Euann.

"No!" The sound barely made it past Euann's lips before his body became compact and morphed. Fur sprouted on Euann's face. Sharp small teeth filled his mouth. Within moments, a gray fox ran from where Euann once stood.

"What? Euann?" Erik asked in confusion as his brother darted down the stairs.

"Shif'!" Jewel pointed at Erik.

"Stop her," Murdoch ordered. He ran after

Euann only to stop at the bottom of the stairs as Euann continued into the dining room.

Erik dropped the phone. Andrea watched from above as he tilted his head back. She could see his transformation better than she had Euann's. His eyes glowed. Fur grew from his flesh. An awful cracking noise sounded as his jaw displaced. He made a loud noise as his hands lifted. Fingers widened into paws. The sound changed from the cry of a man to an animal's growl.

"Sorry, laddie." Murdoch tossed his hand in Erik's direction. Yellow lights erupted around Erik, freezing him into place.

"Kitty!" Jewel appeared next to Erik clapping her hands. His vicious mouth was opened wide but it didn't scare the child as she began petting his head. "Nice kitty."

"What is all the commotion?" Margareta appeared in the doorway.

Andrea motioned at Raibeart, holding her throat as she choked for air. He turned his blow dart on her, popping the balloon. Oxygen rushed in and she gasped, even as her body plummeted toward the hard marble below.

"Murdoch," Raibeart shouted.

"On it." Murdoch appeared below her. He held up his hands, padding her fall with a rush of blue light before catching her in his arms. "There we go." He laid her gently on the floor. "Safe and sound. Take a moment and catch your breath."

"Iain get down here at once," Margareta ordered the bird.

"Jewel? Where did ya put Andrea?" Kenneth appeared behind his mother. His movements were stiff. The lipstick had stained his face.

"I'm fine," Andrea croaked, breathing heavily. She still felt dizzy but was thankful to be on the ground.

Iain swooped his mother as she continued to yell at him.

"Jane is on her way," Murdoch assured Margareta while going to stop Jewel from climbing on top of the kitty's back. He lifted her into the air. The child squealed with delight. "That's enough of that, dear heart."

"Iain, I said get down here." Margareta held out her arm to create a perch for her son.

"Da, shif'!" Jewel commanded, wiggling to be set down. Murdoch adjusted her in his arms.

Kenneth touched his chest, rubbing his hand over the scars beneath his shirt. "Jewel, ya are not to—"

Jewel giggled. A soft glow came from where she touched Murdoch's cheek. Murdoch paled. Jewel's skin shimmered.

"Da, shif'!" she repeated.

Andrea stood from the floor.

Kenneth's eyes met hers in a panic. He pressed his hand flat to his chest. His skin reddened and swelled like an allergic reaction. He took several deep breaths, his chest puffing further with each intake of air. As his body widened, he lost about a foot of height.

"Incoming! Hide the breakables," Raibeart yelled from above.

Kenneth's eyes didn't leave hers, even as they changed shape. His nose and mouth elongated. His arms and legs became thick with muscle. Brown fur covered the distended flesh.

Murdoch fell to his knees, managing to put Jewel on her feet before he tipped over on his side. Margareta ran to Murdoch, cradling his head as she studied his face.

Kenneth transformed into a giant brown bear. He lifted his head and roared, an ugly raw sound that shot terror through Andrea.

"*Rar!*" Jewel swung her head back, mimicking her father.

The child started to go toward the bear. Andrea sprang into action. She darted for Jewel, sweeping her up with one arm as she ran toward the stairs. Jewel squealed, clearly unaware of any danger.

As they reached the top of the stairs, Andrea glanced back. Kenneth had started to follow them. His paws were on the staircase as he looked up. Erik remained frozen. Murdoch sat on the floor holding his head. It appeared as if Jewel had drained him of his magick. Iain soared around the ceiling. Euann was nowhere to be seen.

Raibeart appeared next to Andrea and whispered to her, "Phoenixes are playful little things, aren't they? All mayhem and madness."

"Jewel," Andrea said sternly, "no more shifts. Turn everyone back."

The child's smile fell.

"Jewel, do it or you'll have to go into time out." Andrea wasn't sure how she'd put a magickal toddler in time out, but it was worth a try.

"I don't think she knows what that is," Raibeart said.

Jewel tried to smile at her. Andrea forced her expression to stay firm. It wasn't difficult considering there was a bear on the staircase.

"Raibeart, get her bracelets," Andrea said.

Raibeart gave a small salute before running to —*hopefully*—do as she asked.

"Playtime is over," Andrea stated. She put the girl on her feet and held her arms at her sides so she couldn't point at anyone else.

Jewel's eyes teared a little and her smile fell. A glow of magick caught Andrea's attention. Iain dove for the floor, landing as he became human once more. Erik returned to his human self, but remained in the cat's pose, still frozen. Andrea turned to the stairs. Kenneth stared up at her, his lips parted as if he wasn't sure what to say. The orange-red lipstick was gone.

"Here." Raibeart returned, handing Andrea the bracelets.

She slipped them over the girl's ankles as she'd seen Kenneth do. Even with the bent metal they were still too big.

"Thank you, Jewel," Andrea said.

Euann appeared in human form in the dining room door. Everyone looked back to normal for the most part excerpt for Murdoch who remained seated on the marble floor.

"Euann, get Cait," Margareta ordered. "Tell her that her husband needs to borrow some of her magick."

"Andrea, how…?" Kenneth came to the top of the stairs.

Andrea cradled Jewel in her arms and stood. She was careful to keep the bracelets on the girl's legs. To Kenneth, she said, "This is insanity. You need smaller bracelets for her. This family cannot be held hostage to the whims of a toddler. There is a real danger trying to get into this house. What would happen if it chose to attack two minutes ago?"

"She's never done anything quite on this scale before," Kenneth said. "We weren't telling her that some of us were shifters. I don't know how she found out." He frowned, looking past Andrea to Raibeart. "What did ya do?"

"Story time?" Raibeart gave a small shrug.

"Uncle Chin-ken fly," Jewel informed her father.

"I think it's time to play the sleeping game." Kenneth approached. Andrea studied his hands, unable to help thinking of the paws. "See if you can beat me—"

Jewel relaxed in her arms, instantly asleep.

"Ma, is Murdoch all right?" Kenneth asked.

"Just a little drained," Margareta answered. "Nothing Cait can't heal."

"How do we get smaller bracelets?" Andrea insisted.

"Trina." Kenneth frowned. "Jewel's grandmother."

"The mountain witch?" Andrea clarified.

Kenneth nodded.

"Then that is who we need to talk to," Andrea said.

"I haven't been able to get ahold of her."

Kenneth took Jewel from Andrea's arms and carried the child toward her bedroom. "I've tried. I've left messages. I've even mailed her a letter. She's not exactly one ya can call on the phone for a chat."

"Then we go to her," Andrea stated. She didn't follow him to Jewel's bedroom as he went to lay the child down.

Andrea looked from the balcony at the people below. Cait sat by her husband, running her hands over his chest as he lay on the floor. The woman leaned on her hip with her ankles crossed to the side. The prim and proper lady couldn't have been comfortable in her A-line skirt and blouse.

"When you're done with him, you can take the house arrest off Kenneth," Andrea called down to Cait. They'd briefly met when she came to get Jewel for a picture. She seemed proper and polite, but beyond that Andrea didn't get much of a read off the woman.

Margareta opened her mouth as if to protest.

"It's not up for discussion," Andrea preempted. The fact that her lover had just turned into a bear was still freaking her out. She waved her hand to encompass the hall. "This nonsense cannot happen again."

"It's only a little magick," Margareta

dismissed, as if such things were a common occurrence. "She's playful. All magickal children are."

She eyed the family as they stared at her. Even Murdoch, shaky and pale, wore the same expression. They thought this was normal. What kind of life did they live to think being transformed into an animal at the whim of a toddler was normal? Or being put in a bubble? Or flying with plaid wings? Or kidnapping people through portals, if that's who had done it?

"You may think it's cute now, but what happens when she's a rebellious teenager? When hormones rush in?" Andrea couldn't imagine what she would have done as an angsty teenager if she'd been able to bend everyone to her will. She could guarantee that it would not have been good.

Their expressions fell by varying degrees.

Raibeart put a hand on her arm. Even he looked sad. His voice was low. "Love, she's a phoenix and could be reborn at any time. She might not make it that long. We want to enjoy her while we are—"

"I don't accept that," Andrea interrupted.

"Ya weren't there when…" Raibeart looked away.

Andrea took a deep breath, releasing some of the tension she carried as she understood what was happening. They were all terrified of losing the child and were handling it in different ways. Raibeart spoiled her. Margareta tried to lock her away from danger so she could always be watched over. They created a private world for the girl, here in the mansion. The others helped support that world in varying degrees.

"If Jewel were sick, you'd take her to a doctor, right?" Andrea didn't wait for an answer to her question. "You'd get her the medicine she needed to be healthy and safe. Jewel is magick and she needs guidance with that, and we need to help her in the same way we'd help her if she were sick. She needs to see this Trina woman. It sounds like Trina raised a daughter who was a phoenix. She'll know how to help Jewel."

"Magick is not a disease. Those witches can't be trusted," Margareta argued. "They—"

"We don't have a choice." Cait reached toward Margareta, not touching her. "Andrea is right. Not about the sickness analogy, but about helping Jewel. That girl has more magick than all of our children combined."

"The witches attacked our family," Margareta said. "They're careless."

"And they raised a phoenix to adulthood." Andrea began to feel like she was making decrees to the people below from her balcony perch. It wasn't a pleasant feeling.

When she turned to look at Raibeart, she saw Kenneth standing in the hall behind him. He gave a small nod.

"You hired me to be the nanny and take care of Jewel, so that's what I'm doing. We're leaving in the morning," Andrea said to the women below. Sure, it wasn't in the nanny's purview to dictate what happens with a child, but it was obvious she'd been drawn to this family to help them. "I'd prefer for Kenneth to take the road trip with me, but I'll take Jewel on my own if I have to. Now, excuse me, I have to check on Jewel."

Andrea didn't give them time to respond as she hurried out of their sight. She hoped they didn't call her bluff.

Chapter Fifteen

Freedom.

Kenneth took a deep breath. He knew his mother meant well and thought she was doing the right thing for her family, but it had been way too long since he'd had fresh air that didn't come from standing on the top of the mansion roof or an opened window. No amount of arguing had persuaded his ma to let him out of the house. It had taken the determination of an outsider to convince Cait and his ma to lift the spell.

Margareta was not pleased about them leaving. Euann admitted she'd asked him to put a tracker on their vehicle so she could keep an eye on where they went. If Kenneth was surprised about anything, it was the fact his ma hadn't put trackers on all of the vehicles before now.

"It would be so much easier if we could use a portal," Andrea said as she steered Iain's SUV down the driveway from the house. She insisted on driving so Kenneth could keep an eye on Jewel in the car seat. They could have flown, but Jewel in the sky seemed like a risky idea.

"She's too young. If I asked her to take us to West Virginia we might end up on the moon. She has no concept of geography. I think her bringing ya to us was more of a primal instinct than a conscious one." Kenneth didn't want to encourage magickal use one minute and then forbid it in the next. Jewel was too young to understand.

"So you think the portals are her doing?" Andrea asked. "And not…?"

Her words trailed off and she gave him a meaningful glance.

"I'm fairly certain. Jewel has a way of bringing people she needs into her sphere."

The vehicle had a tv screen in the back of the driver's seat and the sound of cartoon voices came from the speakers. Since Jewel did not see a lot of television, it was a treat for her. His only rule was no princess movies. That had not gone well in her last life. She'd magickally forced the entire family to be part of a royal ball and eat nothing but cookies. The fuzzy creature teaching her the alphabet seemed safe enough.

He glanced back to make sure the bracelets were still sewn onto her pink tights. Jewel giggled at the tv screen. She was such a happy child. In that he'd always been lucky.

"Since it's nearly a thirteen-hour drive, not including stops, I thought we'd push through as far as we can today. Maybe staying the night in Indiana," Andrea said, glancing in the rearview mirror as they neared the highway on-ramp. "Is that your brother following us?"

Kenneth turned in his seat. He let his eyes shift to better see into the car following them. "Aye. Erik, Euann, and Rory from what I can tell."

He reached for his phone on the console between them. Waving his hand over it, he made it dial without touching the screen. Seconds later Rory answered.

"Before ya get your panties in a twist," Rory explained stopping Kenneth from talking, "it was either us or Aunt Margareta and my ma. Ya really didn't think they would let ya travel across the country without backup, did ya?"

"Road trip!" Euann yelled in the background.

"Date crashers!" Erik added.

Both brothers erupted into laughter and teasing.

"My ma sent them after us," Kenneth told Andrea.

"Want me to try to lose them?" She winked at him.

"Tempting," he agreed before saying into the phone, "Call if ya need to stop."

Kenneth hung up on his cousin.

"I can't say I'm shocked," Andrea said. "I honestly didn't think she'd let us leave this morning."

"Ya made a compelling argument." Kenneth gave a small laugh and reached a hand to rest on her thigh. "I have never seen anyone stand up to my mother like that. I can't tell if she likes ya or wants to turn ya into a lawn ornament."

"I'm guessing she'd rather see me as a pink flamingo than your girlfriend. She insisted I stay on that cot in Jewel's room last night. It was most likely to keep me away from you. And, before we left, she did warn me not to be a bad influence on you."

Andrea smiled at him. Jewel giggled at her cartoon.

Kenneth removed his hand from Andrea's leg. He turned his attention to the field outside his window. A strange feeling came over him. Movement drew his eyes to the road as a car passed. The man driving gave him a small nod while a woman and two kids sang a lively song. It was a tiny movement but there was something to the man's contented look as he drove with his family.

This moment with Andrea felt…

Kenneth felt…

Normal.

This felt normal.

And it terrified him.

He wondered what it would be like if Andrea were his wife and they were taking a road trip with their daughter. What if the most significant threat was a flat tire or taking a wrong turn? The desire for that brief fantasy gripped him and he wanted it desperately.

Normal never worked in his family, at least not for long. If he let himself imagine possibilities that could never be, it would only cause severe disappointment later.

"Looks like it's going to storm." Andrea leaned forward to look up at the sky through the windshield. Her hands gripped the wheel, working nervously.

"I'll call Erik." Kenneth grabbed his phone. "He'll make sure we have clear roads. He has a way with the weather."

"He can do that?" Andrea arched a brow. "I see there are some definite perks to dating a warlock." Suddenly, she began to chuckle.

"What?"

"Raibeart called you a bear rug yesterday when you were frozen on the floor." She laughed harder. "And you turn into a bear. I just got the joke. Bear rug."

"I've been waiting for ya to ask me about that. I'm glad to see ya can laugh about it." He put the phone back down, not calling his brother. Upon further consideration, he knew Erik would see the storm and keep it back.

"Don't get me wrong. I was scared when you shifted. I didn't think something like that was possible in real life." She glanced in his direction several times. "And, by your family's reaction, I get the impression that wasn't all Jewel's magick."

"She is powerful enough that in time she could eventually change people into animals, but this time it was easy since my brothers and I carry the ability inside us. Jewel forced it out."

"And Murdoch?"

"She borrowed his magick to amplify her own to get past my protection." He touched his chest. That was a new trick, and one of the few reasons why Margareta finally caved and let him go. If Jewel didn't have to listen to her father, then raising her would become all that more difficult.

"He looked better this morning." Andrea didn't sound convinced. Murdoch had been shaky and weak and had stayed far away from Jewel.

"I think he's scared of her," Kenneth glanced back at Jewel. His daughter's head rested against the side of the car seat as she stared at the screen. "This wouldn't have happened if I was able to raise her alone like before. She can't take from me and would never have learned that trick. Now she's even more dangerous."

Andrea reached over, placed her hand on his, and squeezed. "I'll help you figure this out. I promise. You're raising a sweet kid."

His phone rang and he answered Euann's call.

"Rory has to pee," Euann announced.

"We haven't even been on the road for an hour. Tell him to be a big boy and hold it." Kenneth hung up.

"Everything all right?" Andrea asked.

Kenneth chuckled. "Probably not. It's a MacGregor road trip. There are so many ways this can go sideways on us."

The storm clouds churned parallel to them along the road. Erik was doing is part.

Euann's car appeared by the driver's side window. Rory held up a handwritten sign. *"Hot dogs?"* He pointed forward to a billboard that boasted two-foot hot dogs drenched in Wisconsin cheese sauce.

Andrea laughed and nodded at Rory before

giving him a thumbs up. Rory pumped his fist excitedly in the air and then blew her a kiss.

Kenneth sighed, shook his head, and muttered, "That's not good."

"What? It's fine," Andrea said. "We can stock up on road snacks."

"That's not why I'm worried. My sister can materialize food from pictures and well..." He watched the giant hot dogs on the billboard as they drove by them. "I have a feeling Rory is going to steal that sign later. He won't be able to resist a twenty-foot hot dog."

Chapter Sixteen

Andrea was used to long hours on the road, but the time passed much easier with company. There were times she forgot about the storm clouds chasing them. With the binding bracelets, Jewel was forced to behave. Well, at least behave like a normal child. On one of their gas station stops, Jewel tried to bite a lady who stuck her finger in her face after making a snide comment about how the bracelets sewn onto the tights were "an interesting choice for a child." To be fair, Andrea kind of wanted to bite the rude woman too.

Kenneth wore jeans, but the others were in kilts. The amount of attention a group of handsome Scots drew didn't faze them, and the MacGregor charm appeared as natural as breathing. They even posed for pictures.

"They do realize they're going to be made into internet memes later and put in private groups where ladies can ogle them, don't they?" Andrea said to Kenneth as he took the long way around a snack aisle to avoid the camera phones.

"I'm pretty sure Rory is counting on it," Kenneth answered. "And what do ya know about these private internet ogling groups?"

"My sister Annie loves them."

"Sure. *Annie* loves them," he teased.

"But seriously, why don't you wear a kilt?" Andrea gave him a playful look and glanced down to his legs. There was something to be said about the sexy outfit.

"You'd like that, wouldn't ya?" Kenneth laughed.

"Uh, yeah. Of course I would." Andrea nodded.

Kenneth chuckled. "I stopped when Jewel was born the first time. It tended to draw a lot of unwanted attention. Though, since ya asked, I'll be happy to pull it out of storage for ya."

Besides the cheesy hot dogs, Rory, Euann and Erik bought enough candy throughout the day to fuel a small sugar army. She was glad they were in their own car.

There were a few times she saw the vehicle swerving in her rearview mirror. Thankfully the highways were clear of other cars for most of the trip. When she'd slowed to check it out, she saw what looked like a playful argument. Kenneth didn't appear concerned.

Several times she caught Kenneth staring at her with a questioning expression on his face. She wondered what he was thinking but didn't ask. Conversation flowed smoothly between them. He told her of living in Oklahoma, and how Jewel in her last life had forced a woman to kidnap her and drive them to Green Vallis. Cora married Euann and opened the local public library, so it had worked out well. Andrea had yet to cross paths with the woman.

Turning someone into a kidnapper was much more creative than how Jewel compelled Andrea to come to the mansion. Kenneth was right. Jewel's magick seemed to answer her needs without the child being able to articulate them herself. Was it possible Cecile was merely Jewel's magick gone awry, and nothing else?

Andrea told him of her childhood, of her sisters, of the day her parents died and how she'd felt so alone. Without fully realizing it, she'd been searching for something, a missing piece. She didn't say it out loud, but that feeling hadn't lessened until she'd come to the MacGregor mansion. Being with Kenneth felt right.

By the time evening darkened the sky, Jewel was becoming fussy in her car seat. Kenneth had taken over driving and he followed signs to a hotel boasting an on-site restaurant and indoor pool. The storm clouds had not lessened as they made the journey, but they didn't come closer to the cars.

"I'll have Euann grab our bags," Kenneth said as he pulled into a parking spot. "Are ya all right taking care of Jewel while I check us in?"

"No problem." Andrea reached for the handle but the door opened before she could touch it.

"We should get inside." Rory reached for her arm to help her out of the car. "Erik is tired from holding back those clouds all day, so he's going to let the storm run itself out."

As if to prove his point, the winds picked up, bringing with it a chill.

Andrea helped Jewel out of the car seat and carried her into the hotel. Once in the lobby, she set the girl down to let her stretch her legs. Jewel took off running down a long hall. The child's small feet thudded on the carpet.

"I got her," Andrea said, hurrying after Jewel. They left Kenneth by the check-in counter.

The child stopped at a glass door and pressed her face against it.

Andrea slowed her pace. "What have you found—?"

Before she could finish her sentence, Jewel pushed the door open and ran inside, yelling excitedly, "Bat!"

Andrea saw the indoor pool through the glass door. "No, Jewel, stop!"

Jewel ran straight off the side of the pool and landed in the deep end with a splash. Andrea's heart nearly stopped and she jumped in after her. The cold water hit her skin. She managed to grab the sinking child by the waist and pull her back to the top.

Jewel broke the surface with a cough.

Andrea gasped for air. She swam them toward the shallow end, only pausing when she could stand. She turned Jewel to get a better hold on her.

Jewel coughed again, looking stunned that she had not automatically stayed above the surface. One could imagine she was not used to being in the water with her powers bound and had never been taught how to swim on her own.

"You're okay," Andrea whispered, pushing back the child's hair to see her face. She wasn't sure if she was soothing the girl or herself. Her heart felt like it was lodged in her throat. "You're okay."

"Jewel?" Kenneth's panicked voice preceded him as he appeared in the doorway.

Jewel's eyes teared and she began to cry. The belated tears seemed to indicate she was reacting to her father's emotion more than what had happened. Andrea walked her to the edge of the pool. Kenneth grabbed the wet child from her and held her close.

"I'm here, love, I'm here." Kenneth carried her away from the pool.

Andrea walked to the corner steps and climbed out. Water dripped from her soaked clothes and hair. She grabbed two towels from a stack and tried to hand one to Kenneth. His angry eyes met hers and she instantly withdrew her offer.

"Ya were supposed to watch her," Kenneth managed.

"I…" Andrea couldn't get the words out.

"Come on." His tone was hard. He led the way from the pool back to the hall.

"Is everything all right?" one of the hotel staff started to approach.

Andrea nodded and politely lifted a hand to keep the man from following.

The elevator ride was silent except for the soft whimpers of Jewel. Kenneth refused to look at Andrea. She couldn't blame him for his fear, but it was unfair to take out the child's actions on her.

Water dripped on the floor from Jewel's shoe. Andrea shook out the dry towel and pushed it over the girl's shoulders, forcing Kenneth to grab hold of it.

They walked to the room in the same icy silence. Instead of using a room key, Kenneth gestured toward the door. The green lights on the lock lit up and they were able to enter.

Andrea held the door open as Kenneth and Jewel moved past her. By Andrea's traveling standards the room was large—two beds, a television, a long desk and extra chairs. However, by the MacGregor standards the room was probably small and cheap. Someone had left the air conditioner running and the cold air against her wet clothing caused her to shiver.

Once the door closed completely, she said, "I didn't know she would jump into the pool like that. I'm sorry."

"Ya got her out. That's what matters." His tight voice didn't sound like that was all that mattered.

"I can tell you're angry," Andrea insisted. She wasn't going to spend the rest of the trip with this tension.

"Of course I'm angry." He bit his words as he placed Jewel on the floor, keeping his tone even.

Her shoes squished and she giggled, rocking back and forth to make the noise again.

"I promise, I will always do whatever it is in my power to keep her safe," Andrea insisted.

"But that's just it. Ya have no power."

The words felt like a slap in the face. She took a deep breath. "Maybe that's what Jewel needs, someone to teach her how to be normal."

"Now, don't ya—"

"What happens if we're successful? If we put the binding bracelets on her permanently and she can't get out of them? Do you think she understands she can't jump off a balcony and fly with Uncle Raibeart? Do you think she knows not to touch a hot stove or try to breathe water like a mermaid? She had no fear of the pool, and no skills to get out of it. Yes, she's a toddler. Yes, she's playful and sweet. Yes, I know you all think it's just a magickal kid being a kid when she turns you into animals and wants to pet the giant kitty. What happens when she sees an actual big cat, one who is not Uncle Erik, and decides she wants to reach through the cage to pet it?" Andrea's hands shook and moisture gathered in her eyes. "This child doesn't know risk or fear."

"Andrea—" he tried to speak but she held up her hand.

"She could have died." Tears spilled down her

cheeks as the terror of what could have happened overwhelmed her.

Jewel came across the hotel room and grabbed hold of Andrea's leg. Hugging it, she said, "It's okay."

Kenneth started to come toward her, but the sound of someone at the door stopped him.

"Luggage delivery." Rory poked his head inside. He eyed Jewel and Andrea's wet clothes. "Couldn't wait for a swimsuit?"

"Thanks." Andrea reached to take her bag while trying to pivot toward the bathroom door with a toddler glued to her leg. "Come on, Jewel. Let's get out of our wet clothes."

"We're all heading down for food in five minutes," Rory said, as if that would change Andrea's mind about cleaning up.

When the bathroom door opened, Jewel saw the tub and released her leg. "Bat!"

Andrea barely glanced at Kenneth and his cousin as she followed the child into the bathroom. She closed the door behind them.

Chapter Seventeen

The hotel restaurant overlooked the swimming pool. A row of glass windows flanked the booths along one wall. Their round table happened to be situated at a perfect angle so that every time Kenneth glanced past Jewel's head in Andrea's direction, he saw the water.

He couldn't lose a daughter again. His heart couldn't take it.

Kenneth had witnessed the fear on Andrea's face as she carried Jewel through the water. She'd been right. Jewel wasn't prepared for an ordinary world, but what child was? Parents were meant to keep their children safe. He couldn't help but feel like he'd failed his daughter, all his daughters.

No parent should have to carry this much heartache.

Even so, Andrea had not deserved his anger earlier. He didn't blame her. He blamed himself.

Kenneth placed his hand on top of Jewel's head. She smiled up at him, completely innocent and unaware of the turmoil her playfulness had caused. She waved a chicken strip in his direction, offering to share.

"Eh, give me that." Euann reached across to swipe the food.

Jewel giggled. She then reached to grab French fries off Andrea's plate.

"Hey!" Andrea pretended to protest.

Jewel shoved the fries in her mouth, giggling harder.

After dinner, as they went back to the room, Erik and Rory argued over who would sleep on the cot.

"Are they all sharing the same room?" Andrea asked. Erik and Rory's discussion could be heard continuing down the hall.

"There were only two rooms left. Apparently, there is a national carpet salesman conference in town." Kenneth motioned his hand toward their door to unlock it. Lightning flashed outside the window at the end of the corridor. He carried a sleepy Jewel with one arm as she rested against his shoulder.

"Well, we can't miss that," Andrea drawled

sarcastically. "It sounds like the event of the season."

Once they were inside, he laid Jewel on a bed, tucking her beneath the covers. He gestured for quiet before taking Andrea's hand and leading her to the bathroom and shutting the door. The space wasn't exactly the romantic spot she deserved, but it would have to do. He made a promise to himself that he'd make it up to her.

"I know what you're going to say," Andrea started before he could find his words. "I'm sorry. I have a big mouth. I know that. My sisters tell me I'm bossy all the time. I don't mean to be. It just happens when I get worked up. I had no right to tell you how to raise your daughter."

"Thank ya," he managed.

She nodded.

"I mean," he cupped her cheek, "thank ya for caring. Thank ya for saving her life. I'm glad ya were there when I wasn't. Thank ya for speaking your mind and reminding me that I need to start thinking of all the normal risks in Jewels life, not just the magickal ones. Thank ya for standing up to my ma and Aunt Cait. I don't know how ya got them to listen to ya. I've been trying for two years to get them to lift the house arrest. I know ya didn't ask for any of this. I'm sorry I wasn't my best self earlier when I spoke to ya."

"I understand. You had to be terrified that Jewel…" Andrea gave a worried look toward the door. "She's a special girl."

Kenneth brushed his thumb over the corner of her mouth. He'd never seen anyone so beautiful or caring in his life. He'd sensed it in her, even as he'd been frozen like a statue in the front hall of the mansion when Jewel was a baby. The pieces fit. A force beyond them drew them together, compelled her to come to him. Whether it was magick, or fate, or something he could never understand, he knew it was real.

"I'm sorry this is abrupt." Kenneth again touched her mouth.

"Abrupt?" She furrowed her brow, not following his thought process.

"I love ya," he stated.

Her breath caught. "I wasn't, ah…"

"I know I might sound irrational after the fight we just had, but with all the uncertainty we face, I need to tell ya how I feel." Kenneth didn't care. So what if he sounded crazy? "It's like I told ya before. Living with magick is complicated. I have no need for games between—"

Andrea silenced him with a kiss. He realized she didn't say it back, but he hadn't expected her to. Her words had slipped when he'd been frozen on the floor. He'd heard them, even if she wasn't ready to tell him. His love was not conditioned upon hers. That's not how love worked.

What they had was real. Not everything needed to be said to be understood. Humans often worked on a different timeline than immortals. Some things could be felt. The way she touched him, looked at him, and sighed against his lips told him more than words could. She cared for him. She wanted him.

Their heavy breathing filled the bathroom. He rotated her in the small space, pressing her against the sink counter. She pulled at his shirt, lifting it over his head. Her eyes met his, filled with the same passion he carried inside.

The attraction he felt for her was more than magick or spells. He knew what it was like to be entranced. This was not that. Yes, she was as beautiful as any enchantress, and as alluring as any siren, but Andrea did not contrive or manipulate. She owned her imperfections and did not let them stop her. Her human heart beat with an empathy he'd rarely seen. That much had been evident in the way she spoke of her family on the drive, in how she interacted with his family.

How could Kenneth not be in love with a woman like that?

She tugged her shirt over her head and threw it aside before pushing her pants from her hips.

Kenneth let his magick swell. His clothes melted from his body only to appear on the floor in a pile.

He lifted her so that her ass landed on the edge of the sink. Ripe nipples called to his mouth. Cupping her breasts, he drew one between his lips. She moaned as her hands worked against his shoulders, kneading him in her passion. He kissed his way up her shoulder to her neck. When he peeked through his closed lids, he saw her naked back in the bathroom mirror.

She pressed her hands into the counter and lifted her hips. He cupped her ass, drawing his body to hers. The feel of her sex made him mindless with need.

Kenneth turned her so she pressed against the bathroom door and her legs wrapped his thighs. He rocked into her. Nails bit into his flesh, scratching his back and sliding into his hair. He tried to kiss her but their lips did not stay locked with the motion of their bodies.

Andrea gasped, making a small noise of pleasure as she met her climax. It was all the encouragement his body needed. Her release fueled his magick, making him feel as if he could conquer the world. He came inside her, giving himself over to her completely.

Her back slid down the door as he lowered her to the floor. They breathed hard in unison.

A small smile graced her lips as she looked up at him. "That was fun."

He was about to answer when he heard the sound of a door. Her eyes widened. She'd heard it too.

Kenneth gestured his hand up his chest, calling his clothes to cover his body as he reached to open the bathroom door. Andrea darted behind him to grab her clothes. When he went into the room, the door was open. He glanced toward the bed. Jewel was gone.

Kenneth hurried to the door, but instead of the hotel he saw the upstairs hallway of his home. Jewel walked away from him missing the tights where Andrea had fastened the bracelets.

"Kenneth?" Andrea asked. "Who is it?"

Kenneth ran after Jewel, passing through the portal.

"Wait," Andrea said behind him.

His feet hit the MacGregor hallway carpet and he swooped Jewel into his arms. Andrea bumped into his back. In unison, they turned toward the hotel room door, but it had disappeared.

Jewel gave a big yawn and lifted her arm toward her room. "Night, night, da."

In that one instant, the entire day of driving had been erased.

"I…" Kenneth looked helplessly at Andrea.

She wore unfastened jeans, an inside-out t-shirt, and from what he could tell no bra.

"Well…" Andrea shrugged, clearly at a loss. "I guess that solves who has been making the portals. Looks like Jewel wanted her own bed."

Kenneth carried Jewel to her room.

"Who's here?" Raibeart's voice came from the hallway. "Andrea? You're back from your trip already? How long was I asleep?"

Kenneth laid Jewel in her bed and gave her a quick kiss on the head.

"Jewel wanted to come home," Andrea answered.

Going to the hall, Kenneth said, "Raibeart, I need ya to call Erik and tell him to take care of the hotel room for us. Let him know Jewel opened a portal and brought us back here. Make sure he finds Jewel's bracelets."

"A portal? Ya don't say." Raibeart nodded and gave a small laugh. "Playful little thing, isn't she?"

If he wasn't mistaken, there was pride in his uncle's voice.

"What about West Virginia?" Andrea asked.

Kenneth ran his hands through his hair. "Raibeart, tell Erik to keep going. If we can't go there, he'll need to find Trina and get her to come to us. Make sure he knows that we need him to hurry. These portals are new. She's never done anything like this before. With nothing to bind Jewel's powers, I'm not sure we can continue to keep her safe."

"Nothing is going to harm that baby," Raibeart stated, even as he materialized a phone to make the call. "I'll stay with her."

Andrea touched his arm. "Maybe we should have Jewel sleep with us tonight so we can feel if she wakes up."

Kenneth nodded. "Raibeart, Andrea is right. I'm immune and Andrea is human. Jewel can't tap into more magick with us, not like she did with Murdoch. It's safer if everyone else stays away for now."

Raibeart nodded but didn't appear as if he liked the decision. "I'll call Erik."

"Oh and tell him to be careful. The mountain witches don't like visitors," Kenneth instructed.

Raibeart waved his hand as he walked away, holding the phone to his ear.

When they were alone, Kenneth said, "We can't let Jewel out of our sight. If that portal had not led home... If we hadn't seen it... If she would have walked through—"

Andrea tightened her grip on his arm. "None of that happened. She's here. She's safe. We're not going to let anything bad happen. We'll do whatever we need for her to be safe. In a couple of days, Erik will be back with Trina and we'll get this figured out. Get Jewel and bring her to our bed. We got this."

Kenneth nodded. "Ya can sleep first. I'll stay up and watch her."

Chapter Eighteen

A couple of days chasing after an energetic magickal child left Andrea exhausted. Each second Jewel had to be carefully watched. All it would take is one portal and the child could disappear forever. Andrea had no idea how Kenneth managed raising Jewel three times on his own. The portals might have been a new power, but they weren't the only thing of concern.

Though they could technically leave the house, Andrea didn't want to. Thunderstorms raged, slamming the town with a torrential downpour and darkening the landscape under its gloom. Flood warnings were issued and people were told to stay indoors.

Andrea had tried to focus on Jewel and Kenneth, but the cold hand of fear gripped her chest with each strike of lightning and boom of thunder. She remembered all too well what it felt like to be in the swamp, facing Mama Cecile. The entity might not be who she thought, but something had attacked her. That was very real. Hopefully, once they put the bracelets on Jewel permanently, the phantom would go away forever.

She stared at the dark window, watching as light flashed against the wet pane. The fear and coldness she carried since that day would not leave her. So if Cecile wasn't a ghost, and if Jewel hadn't created her to lure Andrea to the mansion, then what was it?

"Andrea?" Kenneth's hand slipped onto her shoulder. He laid next to her on the bed. Cait read quietly in Jewel's room, watching as the child slept. She would get them if the child woke up. "What are ya doing awake? Ya need sleep. Ya can't keep staying up like this."

"I feel it outside," Andrea whispered.

Kenneth shot out of bed, leaping over her to land on the floor before hurrying to the window. Blue lights wound his fingers as if preparing to fight. He leaned against the pane, searching the yard below. Lightning flashed a couple of times before he finally turned back to the bed. He extinguished the magick around his fingers. "I don't see anything."

Andrea hugged the covers against her chest. "It's in the storm." She shivered. Her eyes burned from being awake too long. "Or it is the storm."

Tick. Tick.

The sound was soft, but unmistakable.

"I hear it, ticking like a clock. It's almost constant now." Andrea watched Kenneth come toward her. "I think time is running out. I don't think this storm is going to stop on its own. I think I should—"

"Don't say ya should leave," he interrupted. "Ya belong here."

A tear slipped over her cheek. How could she make him understand? When he looked at her, his expression was so open, so honest. He had said he loved her, and she believed him. She had not said it back—not because she didn't feel it, but because saying the words would make everything permanent. A man like Kenneth would never let her go if he thought she loved him. He would fight whatever came.

Tick. Tick.

As much as she wanted to hope Jewel was the cause of Mama Cecile and it could all go away, she knew that was a lie.

Maybe it was lack of sleep, or perhaps she was finally ready to admit the truth she should have always known. The ticking was a countdown, some cosmic clock warning her that the end was near. The moment Cecile had grabbed her chest she'd known she was on borrowed time. She'd been dying since that night in the swamp. Maybe that borrowed time was simply to give her a chance to stop the devastation of the apocalyptic vision.

Andrea slid off the bed, moving past Kenneth. Lightning came from several spots in the sky, like the fingers of angry gods. It struck above the forest and she watched for the trees to light up in flames. The only reason the entire woods wasn't burning down had to be because of the rain.

Lightning flashed again, only this time instead of returning to darkness she saw the forest in ruins beneath a dust-filled sky. Smoke from dying fires rose into the heavens. The trees were reduced to ashen stumps. The end was near. She felt it's threat like ice water in her veins.

"Andrea?" Kenneth's warm hands on her shoulders drew her away from the vision.

"I don't like storms," she said, letting him guide her back to the bed. He lifted the covers so she could crawl in before he settled next to her.

Kenneth pulled her into his arms and held her close. "The storms can't hurt ya, love. Ya are safe here. I promise."

She wished that were true.

Chapter Nineteen

Andrea inhaled sharply as she felt hands on her face and pressure against her chest. She came from a deep and disoriented sleep. Blinking rapidly, she automatically prepared to swat whatever held her down when her eyes met with Jewel's.

The girl pressed her face close so that their noses almost touched. "It's okay, Andrea."

Instead of swatting, she touched the child's back to hold her as she turned to her side. The child dropped onto the mattress and Andrea took a deep breath.

"Jewel?" Kenneth came running into the room. His eyes met hers. "I'm sorry. She wanted to know where ya were and I tried to tell her to let ya sleep."

"It's okay," Jewel repeated, petting Andrea's hair, as if trying to comfort her. Her words were increasingly easier to understand, so unlike the babbling of that first day.

"What are you doing, cuddle bug?" Andrea suppressed a yawn. "Do you want breakfast?"

Jewel grabbed her face. Her eyes were wide as she said, "It's okay."

Andrea frowned. Lightning flashed but the storm seemed less angry.

Kenneth scooped his daughter into his arms and began carrying her from the room.

"Wait." Andrea swung her legs off the bed and moved to follow them. "Jewel, what's okay?"

Jewel pointed out the open door.

"What are ya doing to my home?" Margareta MacGregor cried.

Kenneth's eyes met hers.

"Do you think your brothers are back with Trina?" Andrea wondered aloud.

They hurried to investigate the commotion. By all accounts, Trina's presence would not be welcomed by Margareta.

"Easy, sugar bee, the spirits spoke and we must listen."

"Aunt Florence?" Andrea darted past Kenneth and Jewel. What was she doing here?

She looked down at the main hall as she

rushed past the railing to the stairs. Ruth was sprinkling brick dust along the base of each window, dirtying the pristine marble floors. Margareta was trying to get to her but Florence was holding up a fistful of charms as if to keep back a demon.

"Aunt Florence, Grandmama Ruth, what are you doing?" Andrea didn't stop until she'd passed Margareta. "Florence, please don't point those at her."

"Are you sure?" Florence cocked a brow. "There's a lot of anger in that one."

"It's not anger," Margareta quipped. She flung her hand and shot a tiny blast of magick at Ruth to knock the jar of brick dust from her hand. "It's irritation. I don't appreciate people breaking into my home and dumping dirt all over the place."

"We have never broken into a place in our lives," Ruth huffed, going after the jar as it rolled away from her. She'd left her shoes by the front door and her stocking feet shuffled on the marble.

In her magickal protest, Margareta actually made a bigger mess as the dust spread over the middle of the floor. Ruth finally reached the jar. She lifted it, shaking the contents to gauge how much was left.

"The cute one let us in," Florence said with a

wink. "Would you rather he left guests out in this rain?"

Andrea gave a small smirk at that. It was impossible to tell which MacGregor her aunt meant by *the cute one*. She lifted her arms to the side and moved to hug the woman. "I have missed you so much. What are you doing here?"

"The spirits told us to come," Florence said.

"They speak and you must listen," Andrea answered.

"So true," Florence agreed. "Besides, we were worried about you. It sounded like you needed us on the phone."

"And you needed cheese?" Andrea asked with a laugh.

"Well, I mean, while we're here and all, might as well stock up," Florence agreed.

Andrea released her aunt so she could hug her grandmother. The familiar embrace of her grandmother combined with the smell of her floral perfume. A tear slipped done Andrea's cheek. "You probably shouldn't have come, but I'm happy to see you."

"Time portals are some pretty powerful magick," Ruth answered. "We couldn't leave you to face them alone."

"I take it these two belong to ya?" Margareta inquired, even though the answer was obvious.

"Ma, behave yourself," Kenneth scolded. He still held his daughter. "We're lucky to have the extra protection."

"Hello, sweet one," Margareta said to Jewel, lightly stroking her back.

"Oh, another cute one," Florence said, flashing a smile at Kenneth. "Who might you be?"

"Grandmama Ruth, Florence, I'd like to introduce you to my boyfriend, Kenneth, and his daughter Jewel," Andrea said.

"Well done." Florence nodded in appreciation. "Any chance he'll put on a kilt later like that other one?"

Kenneth chuckled but inched closer to Andrea.

"Come on, Florence, we have lots to do," Ruth said. "There's a hammer in my purse if you need it. Hang those charms."

"Whoa, hey, wait." Andrea rushed forward to stop her aunt before Margareta had a chance to yell again. "Let me see those."

Florence handed the fistful of charms over. Andrea in turn lifted them toward Kenneth. "Any chance you can help them out? These need to hang from each window."

Kenneth tried to lift his hand, but Jewel beat him to it. She wiggled in his arms and said, "Poof!"

The charms disappeared in a small explosion of light only to reappear floating in front of the windows. Jewel clapped at the good job she'd done.

Kenneth motioned his hand, causing the charms to hook over the sill instead of magickally floating.

"Well, aren't you a special little lady," Ruth said. She held up the jar of brick dust. "Any chance you can poof this into a line in front of each window for me?"

"Oh, that's not—" Andrea tried to stop the request but it was too late. Jewel waved her hands. The jar made a tinkling noise as brick dust flew out of it. Lines formed in front of the windows but they were drawn perpendicular, not parallel.

"Close enough," Ruth said. "Andrea, go fix those."

"Yes, Grandmama," Andrea automatically answered.

"I got it," Kenneth said, sweeping his hand to straighten the lines magickally so she didn't have to.

"Now that is a handy little trick." Florence grinned. "What else can that finger do?"

"Leave Andrea's boyfriend alone," Ruth scolded, swatting Florence's arm.

"I'll find your uncles," Margareta muttered under her breath. "We'll take care of it."

"Of what?" Andrea interrupted, letting the woman know she'd heard the comment.

"We're not taking anyone's memories," Kenneth stated.

"But they saw…" Margareta motioned to Jewel. "And they're throwing dirt around."

"Ya wanted us here, ma," Kenneth said, "so ya got us. This is part of it. You're going to live with Andrea's family's brick dust. A little more protection can't hurt."

"They won't tell anyone anything." Andrea glanced at her relatives. They pointed up at the chandelier and started wiggle-dancing. They laughed amongst themselves. "No one would believe them anyway, not really. They've always been eccentric and are known for telling tall tales."

At least, Andrea always assumed along with everyone else that they had been tall tales. Now knowing the MacGregor family and seeing magick and shifting firsthand she wasn't so sure.

"Let's go find that one in the kilt," Florence said. "He said he wanted to ask me a question."

Andrea took a deep, slow breath. Her aunt had to be talking about Raibeart.

"Make sure ya tell him no when he does,"

Kenneth said to Florence. Apparently, he'd come to the same conclusion. "With my uncle, the answer is always no."

"Why don't we see if we can find ya a guest room first?" Margareta said, trying to gesture for the women to follow her toward the back wing past the kitchen and office library.

"Why? Did you lose an entire room?" Ruth snickered at her own joke.

"I think I'm going to need a map to get around this place," Florence added, good-naturedly. "Andrea, why don't you give us a tour and catch us up on everything that's been happening?"

It sounded like an easy request, but it wasn't. Florence's expression shifted just enough to show she was concerned.

Kenneth nodded when she glanced at him. "Go ahead. Ma and I will get lunch ready, won't we ma?"

He didn't give his mother a chance to argue as he began walking toward the kitchen with Jewel.

"Ruth, Florence, it was very nice to meet ya lovely ladies. I look forward to getting to know ya both," Kenneth said with a charming smile at the two women. "You're welcome to stay as long as ya wish."

Both she and Ruth angled their heads to watch his ass as he walked away.

Florence elbowed Andrea in the ribs. "I can see why ya fell for this one. Well done, child. *Very* well done."

Chapter Twenty

Kenneth loved watching Andrea with Ruth and Florence. The two older women were a handful without a doubt, but they made Andrea smile and that expression lit the entire room. At least, it lit up the room for him. His ma was another matter.

Jewel had instantly taken to calling Ruth and Florence, "Gran-mama," and, "Aunt Gran-mama," in an attempt to mimic Andrea. Margareta stiffened each time the joyous words came out of the child's mouth. At one point, his ma dabbed the side of her eye before she muttered some lame excuse to leave the living room.

Suddenly, Florence reached out and grabbed Ruth's arm. The women sat on the couch with Jewel between them. Her expression fell and she glanced around before settling her gaze on the window.

"It's time," Florence said.

Ruth stiffened and followed her gaze.

Even Jewel's smile faltered as her expression turned serious. She placed her hand over Florence's so they both held Ruth's arm. "It's okay."

"What is it?" Andrea stood from her chair and hurried toward the window. "Kenneth, look."

Andrea reached her hand back without turning. Her fingers moved as if grabbing for him. He joined her at the window. Water dripped down the pane, making it hard to see.

In the distance, the skies had shifted from the storm-grays to include a blood-red light.

"Is it… fire?" Andrea asked, leaning to the side as if a new angle would reveal the answer.

Eerie clouds rolled across the heavens, like the dust kicked up from the hooves of running horses. Only, there were no horses.

"What is it?" Andrea asked.

He wrapped his arm around her waist, not taking his eyes off the sky.

"It's okay," Jewel repeated.

"Andrea, I want ya to take Jewel and hide," he whispered.

"You're coming with us, right?" she demanded.

At that he turned to meet her gaze. "I trust ya to protect her."

"But you're going to be there, right?" she insisted.

She knew the answer. He didn't need to tell her.

"It's okay," Jewel said, louder.

"Kenneth, Andrea," Ruth called in concern.

They both turned to where Jewel was levitating over the couch. She wore a long t-shirt over leggings. The leggings had holes from where the bracelets had been yanked off. Her eyes flashed with flames.

Ruth and Florence backed away from the girl in fright.

"Flo, get the charms," Ruth ordered.

"No, wait." Andrea stepped forward. "It's not a possession."

Ruth and Florence looked as if Andrea were clearly insane.

"She has magick powers," Andrea said. "She's a phoenix."

"Jewel, love, get down," Kenneth ordered. He grabbed the bracelets off the floor and clutched them in his hand.

The flames in Jewel's eyes spread down her

cheeks like tears, trailing down her neck before alighting her entire body. The fire had a pink tint to it.

"No!" Kenneth had seen the flames of rebirth before. He knew what this meant.

Kenneth charged toward his daughter, leaping into the air to catch her and hold her. Her skin burned his clothes and sent him flying back. He caught himself as he landed on the floor.

"Jewel," Andrea called to the child. "It's time to stop. Why don't you come down and we can play a game? Bath?"

Jewel burned brighter. He couldn't lose her. Not again.

Kenneth tried to stand, but his body shook. He felt as if he couldn't catch his breath. His heart tightened in his chest.

"*Nooo*," the ragged cry escaped him more as a groan of pain.

Andrea started toward him.

"What's that?" Ruth asked from the window.

"Someone's pulling up the drive," Florence added.

Kenneth motioned for her to check who was coming.

Andrea changed course and hurried to the window. "It's Erik, Rory, and Euann."

"Is Trina with them?" Kenneth asked.

"I don't know," Andrea answered. "Erik is hanging out of the top of the car with his arms outstretched. It looks like lightning is zapping along his skin. I think he's fighting the weird storm clouds."

Kenneth kept an eye on his floating daughter. He inched toward her, wanting to pluck her out of the air but when he'd tried her magick had repelled him and left him weak. He focused his shifter hearing beyond the window. The sound of a revved engine hummed faintly from outside followed by shouts.

"Jewel," Kenneth tried to stay calm. "It's all right. Please come down."

"My stars, that boy nearly crashed into a tree," Florence exclaimed.

Kenneth insisted. "Is Trina with—?"

Jewel sparked and disappeared, leaving behind glowing embers floating softly to the ground. Kenneth darted forward to see past the couch to look for a baby. She wasn't on the floor.

"Jewel," Kenneth cried out.

"Jewel?" Andrea ran from the room and he could hear her calling for his daughter. "Jewel!"

"She's outside," Ruth yelled after Andrea.

Kenneth stumbled to action. His limbs felt heavy. He dragged his feet, unable to run. He heard the front door open.

"Come on, Junior." Florence grabbed him by the arm and began walking him toward the door. The older woman was surprisingly strong as she propped him up.

This kind of weakness was new. He tried to call upon his magick, but all he managed was a faint stirring that tingled his fingertips.

"What's going on?" Margareta appeared in the doorway to the dining room. She leaned against the frame, breathing heavily. "I don't feel well."

Angus joined his wife, pulling her against his chest to offer support.

"Who turned off the magick?" Raibeart demanded as he appeared behind them. His disheveled clothing looked as if it had come from the dirty laundry pile. His shirt was on backward and inside-out. "I had to dress myself. By *hand*."

Shouting sounded outside. Kenneth continued for the front door. Andrea had left it open and the blood-red light filtered in indicating it was growing stronger.

"Like a mortal," Raibeart added.

"What's going on?" Angus asked, his eyes meeting Kenneth's.

"Jewel," Kenneth answered. Had the child sucked all of their energy to fuel her own magick?

"There we go. Almost there," Florence said.

Kenneth shrugged off her hand when they finally made it to the front door. "Stay inside. You're safer in here."

"Raibeart, check on Cait and Murdoch," Margareta said, going to her knees. "Make sure they're unharmed. And call the children."

"On it," Raibeart acknowledged.

Kenneth stumbled onto the front steps to lean against a column. The bracelets were still clutched in his fist. The car Rory and his brothers had been driving had been parked on the lawn. Skid marks rutted the earth where the tires had slid. Erik's body poked out of the sunroof and he lay across the top of the vehicle. His hand moved weakly, but he did not push himself up.

Everything was cast in blood-red. Andrea stood on the lawn near a hovering Jewel, but she faced away from the fiery child to shield her from a dark shadow.

"You will not have her, Mama Cecile," Andrea yelled, "or whatever you are."

Kenneth tried to reach Andrea but the closer he moved toward his daughter the weaker he became until he fell on the ground. The cobblestone of the drive bit into his skin. He reached his hand toward Andrea, trying to give her the bracelets.

Rory and Euann escorted someone from the

back seat. Even though it had been years, Trina Castelaww looked exactly as Kenneth remembered, down to the same denim jeans and faded tan jacket. Her button-down shirt hung open over a brown t-shirt. The wind blew the long, straight strands of her graying black locks across her face.

She jerked her arm away from Euann. The wind shifted to reveal her irritated expression. That is where he saw the difference the years had brought. Dark half-circles framed the underside of her tired eyes. Her skin pulled against her features as if she had stopped eating. He knew she was somewhere around three hundred years old, but her age should not have marked her face to such an extent.

Euann fell to the ground. Rory stumbled, but then veered to the side to land in the grassy lawn.

The dark shadow in front of Andrea began to take a human form—arms, legs, and a head. Kenneth crawled toward her. He would spend his very last breath trying to defend Jewel and Andrea.

Chapter Twenty-One

If Andrea had thought her night in the swamp was terrifying, then this moment was beyond anything she could define. Smoke had rolled over the landscape, gathering to create the familiar shape of Mama Cecile. Jewel had appeared hovering over the lawn and the phantom had gone directly for her. Andrea jumped between them to block the phantom from reaching the child. She had acted on instinct but hadn't expected her presence to stop Cecile.

Jewel's body threw off an intense heat and she felt like she stood with her back to a bonfire. It contrasted the chill radiating from the phantom.

Tick, tick, tick.

She sensed Kenneth the moment he stepped out of the house. Her attention was already split between the phantom and Jewel, but she managed to glance in his direction. His skin had grayed, as if all the magick had drained out of him, like when Jewel took Murdoch's powers. Was Jewel hurting her family to borrow their magick so she could hover in a ball of flames? Or was it the doing of the phantom who brought with it a bloody storm?

She again glanced to the side. Kenneth's head dropped to the ground. Her heart leapt into her throat.

"Kenneth!" She wanted to go to him, but she couldn't leave his daughter unprotected.

Tick, tick.

The phantom inched closer, not taking a corporeal form.

The large oak by the vehicle parked on the lawn began to tremble. Leaves withered and fell. This was it, the moment she'd dreaded. In the town below she heard the screech of tires before metal crashed into metal. Dark smoke trailed from somewhere beyond the driveway. The shouts that came after the accident were faint, but they reminded her of the vision of the end.

Tick, tick, tick.

This was it.

"You can't hide. You can't seek. You can't find the will to speak," came the disembodied sing-song voices

of the ghost twins as the blurred image of the girls ran past them. Andrea couldn't be bothered with the ghost children at the moment.

"Stay back," Andrea warned the phantom. "I won't let you hurt this child."

A smoke-formed arm lifted, growing fingers.

"I'll go with you. Just leave her alone," Andrea ordered. "If you want someone, take me."

Andrea had no magick, not like the others. She had no way to fight evil smoke. Fear told her to run and hide. Instinct made her stay. She could not abandon Jewel and Kenneth. She cared more for them than she did herself. She had known for years that she was marked for death. This was her curse, not theirs.

The smoky fingers touched her flesh, slipping past her skin toward her heart. She gasped at the pain that radiated through her.

"Geneva Castelaww," a woman shouted. Andrea guessed her to be Trina, Jewel's grand-mother. "What do you think you're doing, girl?"

The phantom turned to the woman.

"Hey, baby, it's me, your mama." Trina soft-ened her tone. "I've been trying to find you."

Geneva's figure began to solidify into that of a young woman. The mask of Mama Cecile slipped away.

"Geneva?" Kenneth's voice was hoarse. He

lifted his head to watch as Geneva took a step toward her mother. "How?"

"Get the bracelets," Trina said. "Put them on."

Andrea glanced at Kenneth but didn't move.

Geneva tilted her head. She stopped moving as Trina held her attention. A hand lifted the motion soft as if reaching for her mother.

"I'm talking to you," Trina said through gritted teeth as she glanced in Andrea's direction. "Get the damned bracelets."

"Oh!" Andrea sprang into action and ran toward Kenneth. She touched his cheek briefly in concern before taking the bracelets from him. She hurried back to Jewel and braced herself as she started to reach into the flames to take hold of the child's limbs. The fire burnt her fingers and she cried out in pain.

"Not on her," Trina grunted. "You. Put them on you. Sacred hallows, doesn't anyone around here know how to do anything?"

Geneva turned her attention back to Andrea. A horrible high-pitched sound left her lips, "*Scrrich!*"

The phantom charged her. The bent metal was too small to fit past her hands to her wrists, but Andrea managed to shove her fingers through it. She screamed as Geneva charged her, standing her ground as she lifted her arms for protection.

Geneva screamed again. Her body slammed into Andrea like a cold wind, forcing her back. The bracelets heated against her palms. The fire of Jewel's body hit her skin.

Geneva turned to smoke. Andrea felt the bracelets pulling the phantom into her hands. The jewelry sucked in the smoke, dispersing it inside her. The fire stopped burning her as the cold took over. It spread up her arms and throughout the rest of her body. The phantom's essence held her in its grasp for what felt like minutes, making it impossible to move. When finally she could gain control of her movements, she dropped to her knees and leaned into the ground. The metal bracelets felt as if they'd been seared into her skin.

Trina's feet appeared before her face.

"What did she do to me?" Andrea asked, trying to look up but only able to see Trina's thighs from her place on the ground.

Trina knelt and met her gaze. "Why did you let it go this far? Did you think you had a choice?"

Andrea lifted her hands. They still clutched the metal. Her mind was numb and she wondered why the woman was asking her strange questions.

Trina pried Andrea's fingers back and gently pulled the bracelets out of her grasp. She lifted the bent metal and frowned. "You know you can't destroy these."

Trina ran her finger through the inside of the bracelets, magickally reworking them into perfect circles.

"Jewel?" Andrea blinked. The heat was gone. She turned to check on the child, worried that she might have been reborn.

Jewel had returned to flesh. She had magickally replaced her outfit with blue jeans and a tan jacket that matched her grandmother.

Trina slid the bracelets over each of Jewel's wrists. The metal tightened into place. The red in the sky lessened, replaced by sunlight. "You'll want to take these off her every once in a while to let her magick run free. She needs to learn to control it just as she needs to walk in the human world as one of them. You'll want to take that time to learn your control over her magick. Better now when she's younger. The teen years are going to be a bitch."

"Jewel?" Kenneth crawled toward them. His strength looked to be returning. "Andrea? Are ya hurt?"

Andrea shook her head, even as she cradled her burnt hands. As Kenneth made it to his daughter, she asked Trina. "What's going on? What did you do to me?"

"I didn't do anything to you." Trina frowned as she stood. "I wouldn't have had to come if you would have just finished the ritual. Instead you nearly destroy the world with this nonsense. What did you think was going to happen if you didn't take your rightful place as her mother? Fate is not something you get to pick and choose. You'd think a warlock would know that."

"I'm not a warlock. I'm not anything magick-al," Andrea said. "I'm human."

Trina chuckled. "Now we know that isn't true, don't we? Who do you think you're talking to? I was who you are once."

"I think you're mistaken. You're a mountain witch, and Geneva's mother." Andrea doubted her situation qualified as the same thing. "I'm a human who knows a little about folk magick."

Trina pulled up her sleeves to show burn marks on her wrists. "How do you think I became Geneva's mother? Like you, I was chosen. A phoenix has to die to be reborn, either into them-selves or into a new child. Their magick finds the mother. I know you might be scared, but you know what you have to do. No more playing around. That baby needs you."

"Trina, what are ya talking about?" Kenneth held Jewel as the child sat on one of his arms. He reached to support Andrea as she rose to her feet.

Rory and Euann helped Erik out of the car. Margareta, Angus, and Raibeart came from inside. Their voices rang in a commotion of questions and concerns.

Florence and Ruth rushed to Andrea's side. They began touching her hair and grabbing her face to see into her eyes.

"I'm all right," Andrea told them, trying to push off their hands.

"Your fingers," Ruth exclaimed.

"I should have something in my bag for that," Florence said.

"Everyone, stop talking for a moment, please." Kenneth shushed them before insisting, "Trina? Was that Geneva? What did she do to Andrea? Where did she go?"

"Do you really not understand?" Trina frowned and shook her head. "I knew warlock magick was nothing compared to the mountain witches, but I would think this is fairly obvious. Geneva performed the death ritual and made you the child's father. The phoenix magick passed on with the death ritual, but the energy from my daughter's life had to go somewhere. It was just floating around, probably building to a furious pitch with being forced to wait for so long for the bracelets to focus Jewel's powers so that her magick could call her new mother."

"The portals came from Geneva?" Kenneth asked.

"If there were portals and if they brought the new mother here, then most likely," Trina agreed. "Or it could have been Jewel. Their magick is connected. It comes from the same ancient place."

"Mama Cecile's form has been chasing me around for two years, terrorizing me. That wasn't someone asking me to watch over her daughter." Andrea wasn't buying this explanation.

"Of course she wasn't asking. Geneva's energy would seek to regain the magick it lost. It's energy, not logic. She found you, probably planted a seed inside you somehow and then followed you here. If you weren't here to absorb it, then it would go straight to the source. Obviously, it's never happened, but it's my belief that such a rejoining would end the world. Or so I seem to remember the visions warning me."

"Ya could have mentioned this when ya gave me the bracelets," Kenneth said.

"Fish need water and the sun will rise tomorrow. Any other obvious things you need me to tell you?" Trina quipped. To Andrea she said, "That child is yours like you birthed her yourself, but if you can't handle it, I can take my grandchild to the mountains with me."

"No," Margareta interrupted, her gaze pleading with Andrea.

"Do you love her?" Trina asked.

The question seemed so simple, and yet Andrea felt the answer. She nodded her head. "Yes."

"Will you protect her?" Trina insisted.

"I think she already proved that," Kenneth said for her. He slipped his arm around her waist and held her against him.

Trina reached inside her coat and pulled out a pouch. To Andrea, she said, "Hold out your hands."

Andrea showed her burns. Trina sprinkled the contents from her pouch over them. "This dirt from my garden will cure almost anything. If you're kind to the earth, she will provide."

"Yes it will," Florence agreed. She held out her hand. "Can I see that?"

Trina handed over the pouch. Florence and Ruth began asking questions about Trina's garden.

Angus went to help Euann and Rory as they assisted Erik inside.

"Take him to the portal mirror. Lydia will want to take care of him at their house. Her energy will help him recover faster than anything we can do," Angus said.

"Good plan. I want to find Cora, too," Euann said. "She's probably at the library. I'll head to town and make sure there's no damage control to be done after that magickal storm."

"What about me? I don't have a wife to help restore my energy," Rory grumped as they went inside.

"Andrea, are ya…?" Kenneth's eyes met hers. His expression held so many questions.

"I love you," she said. "I should have said it earlier when you said it, but I thought I'd have to leave for your protection and I didn't want you trying to make me stay. But when I saw you on the ground, and…"

"I told her, the spirits speak and we must listen," Florence was saying to Trina.

"That they do," Trina agreed. "Can you believe these young'uns nowadays? Can't hear the spirits. Can't see the magick right in front of them. Can't be bothered to put on a couple of bracelets to stop the apocalypse."

"Come here, my little love." Margareta took Jewel out of her father's arms. "Let's get ya inside." Then under her breath, she added, "And into more appropriate clothes."

Raibeart took off running across the yard. "I see ya brats. Get back here."

The two ghost girls zipped into the tree line. Raibeart ran in after them.

"Do we need to help him?" Andrea began to follow.

"He'll be fine," Kenneth dismissed. "We'll find him later. Euann has motion cameras in the forest so we can track him."

"Right," Ruth exclaimed, laughing hard at something Trina said.

"Should we be worried that they're getting along so well?" Kenneth asked.

Andrea started to shake her head.

"Next they'll need me to tell them this bound them as her parents," Trina laughed.

All three women turned to look to where Andrea and Kenneth stood on the driveway.

"Did they just say we're married?" Andrea started to smile at the idea.

"Bound," he said. "But it might be the same thing."

"Might?" she repeated.

"Told you I had a prediction," Florence said to Ruth. "Marriage, baby, chickens. All that is left is the dance of the full moon, a banshee, and burnt pudding."

He pulled her into his arms and stroked her cheek. "I'm a little scared to ask what she means by us being bound. They might keep making fun of us."

"You know, there is one way we figure this out without risking more ridicule," Andrea said.

"How's that?"

"You can just marry me and dance with me under the full moon while I'm dressed like a banshee and we'll serve our guests burnt pudding." They might be insane, but the words felt right. "But I'm going to need you to wear that kilt."

"If you're asking, I'm saying yes," Kenneth said without hesitation.

"Are you sure you don't want to think about it?" she asked, pleasure exploding in her at the idea of being Kenneth's wife.

"A wedding?" Rory said from the doorway, showing he'd been eavesdropping on their conversation. "I know where to get the perfect thing! Euann, hurry up, forget stopping to see Cora. I'm coming with ya. We have to go get that giant hotdog sign so Malina can materialize the most perfect meal. There is going to be a wedding."

Kenneth touched her cheek, drawing her attention back around to face him. "I know what I want. I've said it before. Life is complicated. I see no reason for games when it comes to us."

His lips met hers. Her body hummed with

energy and she knew she was in for many changes, but as long as she was with Kenneth, none of those changes frightened her. This was her destiny. This is where she belonged.

"Hey, Trina, you ever have New Orleans gumbo?" Florence asked. "Ruth makes the best shrimp gumbo. You'll have to come over sometime. We'll trade spells."

Andrea laughed against Kenneth's lips. "Why do I have a feeling that the combination of those three is going to equal a whole lot of trouble?"

Kenneth reached for her hands, gently touching her scarred palms. The dirt had healed them but had not hidden the scars. He kissed each one. "Thank ya for risking your life to save my daughter."

"Our daughter," Andrea corrected.

Kenneth nodded. "Yes. Our family."

Just as he was about to kiss her again, Raibeart's shout came from the tree line. "Retreat! Retreat! Someone stole my kilt."

Ruth gasped. "Oh, my word."

Florence gave a whistle of appreciation.

Andrea leaned to look past Kenneth only to find Raibeart running barelegged toward the house. His backward shirt barely covered his manhood. No one had taken his kilt. It clung to his shirt before falling off into the yard as if he hadn't fastened it correctly when he dressed.

Andrea shook her head with a laugh. "And I thought my family was a handful."

"Wait for me!" Florence moved to follow Raibeart. "Didn't you want to ask me something?"

"Flo, get back here," Ruth scolded. "He wanted to ask me something."

"My family is the handful?" He arched a brow.

Andrea laughed.

"*Our* family," they said in unison.

The End

The Series Continues...

WARLOCKS MACGREGOR® 8: A DASH OF DESTINY

A dash of destiny and a pinch of passion can change everything...

Scottish warlock Rory MacGregor knows something from the supernatural world is trying to kill him. He's not sure exactly what that something is, but it'll make for a fun adventure figuring it all out. Of course, nothing is simple, so when Fate tosses in a dash of destiny to keep him on his toes by way of an enchanting new arrival in town, he's all in.

He just wished she was too.

Life hasn't turned out as planned for Jennifer Greene. After taking care of her sick father for years, she's come to Green Vallis, Wisconsin, for one reason only—a job. She isn't looking for adventure, even if it's by way of a tempting High-

lander in a kilt or men streaking across the coun-
tryside. And she definitely isn't looking for love—
even though love is looking for her.

*Warning: Contains yummy, hot, mischievous MacGregors
who are almost certainly up to no good on their quest to find
true love. And Uncle Raibeart.*

For more information, visit
www.MichellePillow.com

Warlocks MacGregor® Series

Love Potions
Spellbound
Stirring Up Trouble
Cauldrons and Confessions
Spirits and Spells
Kisses and Curses
Magick and Mischief
A Dash of Destiny
Night Magick

More Coming Soon

Visit www.MichellePillow.com for details.

Newsletter

To stay informed about when a new book in the series installments is released, sign up for updates:

Sign up for Michelle's Newsletter
michellepillow.com/author-updates

About Michelle M. Pillow

New York Times & *USA TODAY* **Bestselling Author**

Michelle loves to travel and try new things, whether it's a paranormal investigation of an old Vaudeville Theatre or climbing Mayan temples in Belize. She believes life is an adventure fueled by copious amounts of coffee.

Newly relocated to the American South, Michelle is involved in various film and documentary projects with her talented director husband. She is mom to a fantastic artist. And she's managed by a dog and cat who make sure she's meeting her deadlines.

For the most part she can be found wearing pajama pants and working in her office. There may or may not be dancing. It's all part of the creative process.

**Come say hello! Michelle loves talking
with readers on social media!**

www.MichellePillow.com

facebook.com/AuthorMichellePillow

twitter.com/michellepillow

instagram.com/michellempillow

bookbub.com/authors/michelle-m-pillow

goodreads.com/Michelle_Pillow

amazon.com/author/michellepillow

youtube.com/michellepillow

pinterest.com/michellepillow

Complimentary Material

The Savage King

BY MICHELLE M. PILLOW

Lords of the Var® Book One
by Michelle M. Pillow

Bestselling Catshifter Romance Series

Cat-shifting King Kirill knows he must do his duty by his people. When his father unexpectedly dies, it's his destiny to take the throne and all of the responsibility that entails. What he hadn't prepared for is the troublesome prisoner that's now his to deal with.

Undercover Agent Ulyssa is no man's captive. Trapped in a primitive forest awaiting pickup, she's going to make the best out of a bad situation...which doesn't include falling for the seductions of a king.

∼

About *Lords of the Var*® (Books 1-5)

You met their father, King Attor, in Dragon Lords Books 1-4, now meet the Var Princes!

The cat-shifter princes were raised to not believe in love, especially love for one woman, and they will do everything in their power to live up to their father's expectations. Oh, how the mighty will fall.

∼

The Savage King Excerpt

Kirill watched the door to his bedroom open. He'd been sitting in the dark, trying to relieve the stress headache that had built behind his eyes for the last week. The pain started at the base of his skull and radiated up to his temples until he could hardly see straight.

A heavy responsibility had been thrust on his shoulders, a responsibility he really hadn't prepared himself for, the welfare of the Var people. King Attor had not left him in a good position. He'd rallied the people to the brink of war, convinced them that the Draig were their enemy, and even went so far as to attack the Draig royal family.

Kirill wanted to see peace in the land. However, he knew the facts didn't bode well for it. The Draig had a long list of grievances against King Attor and the Var kingdom.

Before his death, the king had ordered an attack on the four Draig princes, all of which ended horribly for the Var. The worst was when Prince Yusef was stabbed in the back, a most cowardly embarrassment for the Var guard who did it. If he hadn't been executed in the Draig prisons, he would've been ostracized from the Var community. Luckily, Prince Yusef survived or they'd already be at battle.

Attor had also arranged for the kidnapping of Yusef's new bride. The Draig Princess Olena had been rescued, or that too would've led to war. The old king had even tried to poison Princess Morrigan, the future Draig queen, on two separate occasions. She too lived. And those were only a few of the offenses Kirill knew about in the few weeks before King Attor's death. He could just imagine what he didn't know.

Kirill sighed, feeling very tired. He'd known since birth that the day would come when he'd be expected to step up and lead the Var as their new king. He just hadn't expected it to be for another hundred or so years. His father had been a hard man, whom he'd foolishly believed was invincible.

"Here kitty, kitty, kitty." His lovely houseguest's whisper drew his complete attention from his heavy thoughts.

Ulyssa bent over like she expected him to answer to the insulting call. He dropped his fingers from his temple into his lap, and a quizzical smile came to his lips. As he watched her, he wasn't sure if he was angered or amused by her words.

"Are you in here, you little furball?" she said, a little louder.

She wore his clothes. Never had the outfit looked sexier. His jaw tightened in masculine interest, as he unabashedly looked her over. All too well did he remember the softness of her body against his and the gentle, offering pleasure of her sweet lips. She'd made soft whimpering noises when he'd touched her, yielding, purring sounds in the back of her throat. Even with the aid of nef, he was surprised by how easily and confidently she melted into him. The Var were wild, passionate people and were drawn to the same qualities in others. He suspected she'd be an untamed lover.

Too bad she'd belonged to his father first. In his mind, that made her completely untouchable though none would dare question his claim if he were to take her to his bed. Technically, by Var law, she belonged to him until he chose to release her. For an insane moment, he thought about keeping her as a lover. He knew he wouldn't, but the thought was entertaining.

Kirill's grin deepened. Ulyssa strode across his home to the bathroom door with an irritated scowl. It was obvious she didn't see him in the darkened corner, watching her. He detected her engaging smell from across the room, the smell of a woman's desire. It stirred his blood, making his limbs heavy with arousal. And, for the first time since his father's death, his headache relieved itself.

"Hum, maybe I'm looking too high. I'm sure there has to be a little cat door here somewhere. Come here, little kitty. Where are you hiding?"

His slight smile fell at her words. It was easy to detect her mocking tone.

"Where's your little kitty door, huh?" Ulyssa whispered to herself, her blue gaze searching around in the dark.

Kirill grimaced in further displeasure. He watched her open the door to his weapons cabinet. Her eyes rounded, and he thought she might take one. She didn't. Instead, she nodded in appreciation before closing the door and continuing her search for an exit.

She stopped at a narrow window by his kitchen doorway. Her neck craned to the side, as she tried to see out over the distance. Kirill knew she looked at the forest. From under her breath, he heard her vehement whisper, "Where exactly did you little fur balls bring me? Ugh, I need to get out of this flea trap, even if I have to fight every one of you cowardly felines to do it. I've fought species twice as big and three times as frightening. A couple of little kitty cats don't scare me."

If this insolent woman wanted to play tough, oh, he'd play. Curling gracefully forward, Kirill shifted before his hands even touched the ground. He let one thick paw land silently on the floor, followed by a second. Short black fur rippled over his tanned flesh, blending him into the shadows. His clothes fell from his body, and he lowered his head as he crept forward. A low sound of warning started in the back of his throat. He was livid.

To find out more about Michelle's books visit www.MichellePillow.com

Please Leave a Review

THANK YOU FOR READING!

Please take a moment to share your thoughts by reviewing this book.

Be sure to check out Michelle's other titles at www.MichellePillow.com